Cooking

Up

Trouble

Marley Fox

Printed in the United States.

Wagging Tales Press
First Printing, 2025
ISBN: 978-1-962191-08-1

Chapter One

Annie

"You know, chocolate is an aphrodisiac for some people," Trent whispered in my ear. He toyed with the two-carat rock on my finger and smiled—like a hungry lion.

The Murphy bed squeaked like a worried mouse as I wriggled into a more comfortable position. My nose wrinkled beneath the tumbled mess of my auburn curls.

The decadent aroma of baking chocolate saturated the air. John Coltrane melted from the compact stereo I had picked up used, but functional, from the second-hand store. Shadows and candlelight tangoed on the orange peel texture of the wall of my shoebox apartment. I held a warning finger to my lips.

"Shh." I inhaled deeply and sighed.

Trent mulishly ignored me. He held up three fingers in a jaunty little salute. "It's true! Scout's honor! Montezuma supposedly drank three cups a day just to keep," he cleared his throat, "up." He pushed aside a few red curls and nuzzled my neck. He batted those long, dark lashes, feigning innocence at my reproachful stare. "With affairs of state, I'm sure."

"Oh, be patient, will you?" I muttered. "I have to make sure I get it just right."

He squirmed as I licked the tip of my finger. "Please, Annie," he begged.

"Don't talk. You'll ruin it." I pressed a finger against his pouting lips.

"Ruin it?" He rolled away in a huff. "The only thing that seems to be getting ruined here is my concept of a romantic evening for two. Come on, Annie. It's almost Valentine's Day."

"I know," I whispered back. "That's why it's got to be special."

Trent retrieved a bottle of beer that had been lingering on the chipped Formica table. He flopped his lanky frame into a cracked, red vinyl chair and took a tug from the sweaty green bottle.

"Well, I'm not feeling very special," he grumbled.

I raised up on one elbow and lowered the tome I'd been reading—when he wasn't interrupting, that is. *One Thousand and One Ways to Spice It Up!*

Not a bad collection of recipes.

Trent huffed across the room.

"Oh, don't be such a baby." I licked my

finger again and promptly turned the page.

Trent took another pull on the import and returned the bottle to the table with a resounding clunk.

That's it!

I catapulted from the couch. My nose scrunched and my lips puckered. I eyeballed him, mustering any lingering hint of Irish ancestry I still had that could help me put the whammy on him.

Nothing even remotely magical transpired. I growled *sotto voce*.

So much for the luck o' the Irish.

I opted for a more dependable twenty-first-century recourse. I smacked him with a spatula.

He threw up his arms in self-defense. "Ow! What was that for?" he howled. That earned him several additional smacks.

I motioned for him to keep it down. "You do know you can't just throw a couple of ingredients together and call it a soufflé, right?" My words hissed in a forceful whisper. "I can't take chances. I've got to test it before I put it on the menu." Two exasperated hands flew up in the air. "But with all the racket you're making, I'd be better off just calling it a chocolate pancake!"

My gaze swiveled to the oven. By some culinary miracle — in the name of Julia, Gordon, and James — the soufflé still rose, puffing to chocolate perfection. A sigh of relief escaped my lips, and I started straightening my tiny kitchen.

Trent just rolled his eyes. "Not that any customers are there to know the difference."

I whirled to face him, one hand on a cocked hip. "And just what is that supposed to mean?" The other hand brandished a chocolate-covered whisk like a fencing foil.

Trent scoffed. "Come on, Annie. Vitello's is a dinosaur. You don't belong there." He stood, towering over me. He sidled up to me and wrapped his tanned, muscled arms around my trim waist. "Listen to me. You are a superb cook."

"Chef," I corrected. "Cooks have big hairy bellies and bald heads and names like Mel."

He broke into a capped smile that could have fed several third-world nations. "Chef," he conceded. "Point is, you're original and creative. And your talents? Well, they're just wasted at that little hole in the wall."

"I happen to love that little hole in the wall. Louie's done all right by me."

Trent raised one groomed eyebrow. "Could Louie have passed off wheat crackers and processed cheese spread as haute cuisine?"

I half-grinned. "That was pretty good, wasn't it?"

He nuzzled my neck some more, and despite myself, I let out a soft sigh.

"Capers," I babbled as my eyes rolled back in my head. "It was the capers. The culinary panacea."

But then my face clouded over. I pulled away and aimed a seriously intentioned whisk at Trent's immaculate white shirt. He grabbed a well-thumbed *Martha Stewart Living* as a shield.

"And while we're on the subject, sir, don't you ever do that to me again. Do you understand? Call me at the last minute and expect me to prepare a decent dinner for eight? Magic doesn't just happen, you know. It has to be perfectly planned. Organized. You need to make lists!"

I punctuated my lecture by waving the whisk, lobbing an exclamation point of chocolate onto the ceiling. My eyes followed the arc of the goo as it landed with a splat.

"Dang it!"

Grabbing a dishrag, I dragged a chair beneath the offending stain. Trent made no move to help as I teetered on size five tippy toes to erase the mess.

"But, unlike that chocolate, you pulled it off," Trent pronounced smugly, standing just far enough away to avoid any dripping confection. He finally offered a steadying hand as I wobbled.

"That's why I don't understand why you won't quit working at that dive and work someplace where your talents can truly be appreciated," he added, his tone soft but insistent.

I smirked as I stepped down from the wobbly chair. "Don't you mean where I can cushion the collective Parker wallet?"

Trent shrugged. "Dad always says, why not kill two birds with one stone? Shoot the pigeon, but call it squab and charge thirty-six dollars a plate."

"It's so comforting to know I'm marrying a man with scruples. And Vitello's is not a dive. It's a neighborhood landmark. They should put up one of those signs." I absentmindedly lined up my spices, so each name was front and center.

"Yeah. Condemned," Trent huffed. "Seriously, Annie. Come work for Dad. There's a terrific piece of property about to become available. He's going to raze the current building and, in a few months, open the latest link in the Parker restaurant chain. And," he twisted one of my curls around his finger, "he's promised to turn the reins over to me. Sort of an early wedding present."

He grabbed me and pulled me in close. His green eyes sparkled mischievously. "It could be our baby. I'll let you run the kitchen. I'll oversee everything else. We could spend a lot more time together."

His mouth suddenly devoured mine. The abruptness caught me off guard. But before the warm flush of desire could course through my body, I planted two flat palms against his broad chest and pushed away.

"It's a nice thought, Trent." I smoothed a stray curl into place. The idea set my mouth watering. The prospect of running a fully staffed, fully stocked kitchen threatened to crumble my moral resolve like a day-old chocolate chip cookie.

But I shook my head. "I can't do that to Louie. He's like a father to me. He hired me as a head chef when no one else would."

Trent's brow furrowed. "He hired you because no one else would work for that joke he calls a salary. You needed it back then. But you've got me now."

He crossed the room in two long strides. I tagged along behind him.

"I appreciate that, Trent, I do. But I can take care of myself. Besides, after we're married, we'll have years to spend with each other. I don't need to work in one of your father's restaurants for that to happen."

Trent grabbed his jacket from the Murphy bed and turned back to face me. "You could have everything you've ever wanted, Annie. But maybe you don't know what that is anymore."

He grabbed the doorknob and started out of the apartment. I stood frozen, my mouth hanging slack. In a sudden rush, I surged forward.

"Trent!" I called, but it was too late. The door slammed, knocking a poster of the Eiffel Tower askance. My hands dropped to my sides. I shoved them into the pockets of my "Quiche the Cook" apron and shuffled to the oven. Drawing on mismatched potholders, I opened the oven door and pulled out a soufflé as sunken as my mood.

I blew an errant hair from my forehead. Setting the ruined dessert on the stovetop, I collapsed into a kitchen chair. Lifting Trent's abandoned beer, I habitually wiped the wet ring that had formed on the table. I gulped down the last of the warm liquid and shuddered.

"Well," I began. "It certainly can't get any worse."

Of course, that damned Irishman had to put in his two cents.

Damn you, Murphy.

*****

"What do you mean, the restaurant's closing?"

Louie ducked as I waved a baguette in his direction. Curtis, the restaurant's towering Renaissance man, stepped in between us like a human Great Wall of China.

"Annie, relax." Curtis's deep baritone

rolled out like molasses. He plucked the baguette from my hand with the same ease he probably used to dismantle opponents back in his boxing days. "Louie didn't have no choice. Give the man a chance to explain."

Louie peeked out from behind Curtis's bulk. "*Sì, dolcezza.* Give me a chance to explain."

I sniffed, crossing my arms. "Fine. I'm listening."

Louie slumped into a nearby booth, his shoulders sagging. His apron strings, wrapped twice around his narrow waist, emphasized just how much he'd shrunk over the years.

"When I first opened the *ristorante*, she make good money. The neighborhood was good, and people—they bring their *famiglia*, their families, to eat. I watched whole generations grow up. Fall in love. Get married. *Amore!*"

Curtis nodded, as though Louie had just read out a sacred text.

"I see their children play in the water across the street." Louie pointed through the large front window, the graceful golden loops of the Vitello name reversed on the glass. Outside, the fire hydrant stood like a lonely sentry in the twilight.

"But now, the children? They grow up. They move out. The world gets bigger. And the neighborhood—she gets smaller. My customers? They stopped coming so much."

Curtis grunted in agreement. "People ain't got no loyalty no more. Everybody forgets where they came from. They'd rather go to some fancy-pants place where you gotta fork over your kid's college fund for a piece of meat the size of a jellybean, just because some celebrity chef puts his name on the door." He grabbed his mop and plopped it into the bucket of gray, soapy water. "What you need to do, Louie, is spruce up the joint."

I nodded, my curls bouncing enthusiastically. "Curtis is right. Change is good. We can revamp the menu! Maybe something with capers."

Louie shook his head, his expression tired but kind. "It's no use, my friends. I do not have the money. Every day, I try to think of a new idea to keep this place running. But this place? She is old. Run down. Like me."

My heart squeezed. Louie had been a rock for me when I needed it most. I couldn't just let this place die—not without a fight.

"So, you'll let it die?" My voice rose in pitch. "No way. We'll get creative. Maybe we can attract one of those food critics. From *The Times*, even!"

Curtis shook his head like he'd just heard a bad idea. "Saint James? Nah. He's too prissy."

Louie looked up, surprised.

Curtis shrugged. "What? I read."

"Fine, maybe not him," I conceded, "but someone. And we'll feed them food so good, they'll explode." I threw up my hands for emphasis.

Curtis pointed his mop at me. "Just make sure they don't explode all over my fresh-mopped floors."

I chuckled, but Louie didn't. His face was pale, his eyes resigned. "I cannot even afford to pay my workers," he murmured.

Curtis and I exchanged a knowing glance. My last paycheck had bounced, but I hadn't had the heart to tell Louie. From the looks of it, he knew.

He sighed heavily. "I will close the restaurant by the end of the week. Valentine's Day will be our last day."

I stared at Louie, my chest tightening. Vitello's wasn't just a restaurant. It was home— my sanctuary when the world felt too big and too cruel. It was where I'd learned to cook from scratch, how to turn the simplest ingredients into something magical. Louie's recipes, scrawled in his looping handwriting on grease-stained index cards, were etched in my brain as deeply as my own name.

When I first walked through those doors, I had nothing—no confidence, no direction, and certainly no idea how to chiffonade basil. But Louie had seen something in me, a spark I didn't even know I had. Over the years, that spark kindled into a flame. Vitello's didn't just teach me how to cook—it gave me purpose.

The thought of losing it—of losing Louie's laughter bouncing off the walls, Curtis's booming jokes about prissy food critics, the golden glow of the Vitello sign in the window—felt like losing a piece of myself.

But I wasn't going to let that happen. Not to Louie. Not to Vitello's. And not to the part of me that had grown up here. No matter what it took, I'd find a way to keep the doors open.

"Louie…" I trailed off, sitting beside him in the booth. I placed a hand on his shoulder. "What will you do?"

"My cousin Franco has an apartment in Brooklyn. I will stay with him. His feet—they have a terrible smell, but he has the Shopping Channel. It will not be so bad."

"The Shopping Channel?" I cringed.

Louie brightened a little. "*Sì!* He bought this amazing thing…a Thighblaster! It gives you the legs of a movie star in just three short weeks."

I snorted. "Louie, those things don't actually work."

"Oh, *sì*? Then how come Eva Guccione cooked Franco a lasagna after seeing him in short pants at bingo?"

Curtis bellowed with laughter, but I didn't join him. My hands were planted firmly on my hips.

"Don't worry, Louie." I assured, my voice firm. "You won't have to live with Franco and his smelly feet. Vitello's isn't going anywhere. I'll figure something out. I promise."

Louie's eyes softened, the weight of his worry lifting just a little. "*Grazie, dolcezza.* You have a heart bigger than this whole neighborhood."

Curtis gave a firm nod, crossing his arms over his massive chest. "You got this, kid. And you know I'm here if you need me." His grin widened. "Just don't ask me to cook."

Louie patted my hand and gave me a weak smile, but his eyes betrayed his doubt.

As Curtis dipped his mop back into the bucket, I stared out the window at the fire hydrant, willing inspiration to strike. I didn't know how I'd save Vitello's, but I knew one thing: I'd fight with every ounce of me to keep those doors open, no matter how impossible it seemed.

Chapter Two

Jordan

I believe in multitasking. That probably explained the cell phone on one shoulder, the hot dog in my right hand, and the left-handed grip on the steering wheel of my rental car while I tried to read the scrawled address on a scrap of notepaper — the one staring back at me, a reminder of why I'd left everything behind for this wild goose chase. And now, thanks to one wayward dog, I might not even make it there.

It might also explain why the canine that shot out into the middle of the street escaped my notice until I practically ran over it.

"Cheese and crackers!" I dropped everything and yanked the wheel abruptly to the right.

The cell phone flew south.

The paper flew east.

The mutt ran west, narrowly escaping a brutal introduction to the car's front fender.

The nearby fire hydrant, however, remained entirely stationary and rooted firmly to the curb. As I scrambled to determine where the dog had gone, the car made a nasty crunching sound. I tried to remember if I had accepted the rental clerk's offer of collision insurance, but all that came to mind were eyes the color of a clear Kansas sky.

The crash with the hydrant halted the forward motion of the car, but I continued headlong in corroboration of Newton's law. I cursed Mrs. Wilson's tenth-grade science class. Until that point, I had been blissfully unaware of Newton's First Law and wondered what kind of validation this Newton guy had needed so badly that he felt compelled to posit not one, not two, but three laws. The apple fell. End of story. I was validated just by being Jordan.

Presently, I would have been happier being anybody but me, as my head smacked into the steering wheel, tattooing my brow with a sizable gash. The horn pealed into the night, whipping the neighborhood pooches into a howling frenzy.

I slowly lifted my head and squinted through the windshield. Figures danced in and out of focus. I couldn't determine whether the cascading hydrant water was to blame or the lump on my noggin' was the more likely culprit. A hesitant hand reached up to my forehead, and I winced. I drew back blood-stained fingers. Or I suppose it could have been ketchup from the convenience store hot dog that had slid off the dash.

"Hey, buddy? You okay?"

I heard a deep, booming voice. "Yeah. No. A dog." I twisted awkwardly, my knee stuck under the steering column, my foot smashing into a crumpled chip bag as I tried to pull free.

"Yeah, your dog's right there. Damn fool was having himself a four-course meal instead of watching where he was going," the deep voice grumbled.

I wobbled a heavy head. "No. Dog. Furry."

"Well, yeah. It's got a little carpet fuzz on it, but what do you expect? You were just in an accident. Fella don't even know what hit him."

I sighed.

I guess we aren't in Kansas anymore, Toto.

And here I was without a tour guide.

Suddenly, one face came into startling focus. It hit me like a gut punch, pulling memories I'd long buried to the surface.

The surrounding neighborhood faded into a blur. I wasn't thinking about the wreck or the dog anymore. One name rose to the surface of the chaos, sharp and impossible to ignore.

"Annie?" I whispered, barely audible before the darkness pulled me under.

Chapter Three

Annie

I scrambled my first egg at the tender age of two. Of course, as Granny McGowan later explained, eggs cooked much better when cracked into a frying pan and not on the floor. When I recognized the handsome, rugged features of Jordan Shaw, I instantly imagined I knew what that scrambled egg had felt like.

Mixed-up, runny, and definitely headed for the frying pan.

My legs wobbled and threatened to topple me into the pooling water from the broken hydrant. Curtis reached out two cannons and caught me under the arms.

"Whoa, now! You okay, darlin'?"

I shook my head, forcing the Jelly inside to congeal into a single, coherent thought. "Yep."

Curtis eyed me dubiously. "You don't look 'yep'. In fact, you look kind of like last week's special."

I flipped through my mental recipe

Rolodex, trying to remember just what last week's special had been. Oh, yeah. *Pâté á la Râpure*. A traditional Nova Scotian dish made with fowl and an insane eight pounds of potatoes. I seem to recall a surplus of potatoes in the kitchen that week. The dish was delicious, but visually, it was about as exciting as watching paint dry. Gray paint.

I definitely felt gray. If we were being honest, I felt downright ashen.

Why did he have to show up now?

My breath hitched as I looked closer. It couldn't be — Jordan Shaw? Why now? Why him? My chest tightened with the kind of nostalgia that wasn't warm and fuzzy — it was sharp and cold, like the edge of a broken plate. I hadn't thought about Jordan in years — not since the day I packed my knives, turned off the oven, and walked out of his life without looking back.

"Really, Curtis. I'm fine."

The big man raised a quizzical eyebrow but let the matter rest. "You know this young fella? 'Cause he seems to know you."

I considered Curtis's question. Seeing Jordan again wasn't just a blast from the past — it was a full-on hurricane. Every memory I'd buried came rushing back, tangled in regret and questions I'd never dared to answer.

I chewed on my thumbnail. "Know? Know

how? Do you mean intimately? I mean 'know' is such a relative term. Not that we're related or anything. Well, we could have been. Related, that is. Not intimate. Not that it's any of your business and frankly, Curtis, I'm surprised you would even mention such a thing. I mean, really!"

Curtis stared blankly. The urban cry of sirens gave the howling dogs a run for their money.

"Oh, look. The ambulance. I should go. They'll probably want someone to ride in the back, or something. You know. Fill out paperwork. Known allergies. That sort of thing."

"Uh, huh." Curtis nodded knowingly. I scrambled toward the approaching ambulance. I hovered behind the paramedics like a nervous sous chef watching a first-time trainee handle an omelet. Every strap they tightened and every question they asked had me chirping anxious instructions, which they politely ignored.

"Not too tight!" I waved.

"Ma'am? Are you related to the victim?"

I volleyed a glance between Curtis and the woozy Jordan. "Yes. Yes, of course I am. I'm his fiancée."

The big man's jaw fell slack. Curtis's jaw dropped like I'd just declared myself the queen of England. "Fiancée? Well, I'll be damned. I suppose you're gonna tell me you're Lady Whistledown

21

next. Do say hello to the Duke of Hastings and don't forget the garden party with the Featheringtons after."

"Don't worry! I'll be fine, Curtis!" I called as I clambered into the back of the ambulance, waving over the heads of the gathering crowd.

Chapter Four

Trent

I lifted the comb to my hair and thought
better of it. Why mess with perfection? At thirty-
three, I didn't look a day over twenty-five—a fact I
attributed to eating right, two and a half hours in
the gym daily, and maybe a minor cosmetic
enhancement or two. The latter, of course, was
kept in strictest confidence by my plastic surgeon.
Doctor-patient privilege and all.

I justified the artifice by reasoning that my
chosen profession demanded it. Parker restaurants
meant high profile. Celebrities rubbed elbows
with heads of state and sometimes more than that
in the darker booths. That was exactly the point.
As manager at the flagship restaurant, it was my
job to cater to people whose approval shaped
industries. And that required a certain level of
familiarity with beautiful, powerful people.

And it takes one to know one.

No crow's feet or sagging jawline for me.
No, sirree, Bob. I gave a backhanded pat under my

chin and reached for the Ralph Lauren.

Only the classics.

I splashed on some cologne and secured the top button of my shirt, stepping from the marbled vanity area into the expansive main bedroom. A charcoal gray sports jacket lay on the king-sized bed, the only dark spot in the white-on-white decor. I smiled. The jacket had been a birthday gift from Annie. She had probably spent more than several paychecks on the single item, but she understood quality.

That's what I'd always admired about Annie. Her attention to detail, her unwavering sense that everything had to be just so. She wasn't just perfect for me—she completed the life I'd always envisioned.

And yet, sometimes, I wondered if she saw the same future I did.

There were moments—fleeting but sharp— where I caught hesitation in her eyes. Like she was watching a different path fork off in the distance, a road I couldn't—or wouldn't—see. She had never said as much, but there were times I suspected that if I hadn't proposed exactly when I did, she might not have accepted at all.

I pushed the thought away. She said yes. That's all that mattered.

I had been standing in line at the corner coffee Mecca, waiting for my ritual tall skinny decaf latte, when I first saw her. A commotion broke out at the counter, centered on a curly, red-haired minx critiquing the mark of foam on her espresso macchiato.

"The milk has to be frothed to at least 140 degrees, otherwise it collapses too soon," she explained, her voice edged with exasperation. "And you can't just dump it in — you have to swirl it."

The barista, a kid barely out of high school, blinked at her with the vacant stare of a cud-chewing bovine.

She wasn't wrong.

And she didn't back down.

The barista may not have cared, but I found myself enthralled. Her Grace Kelly profile, the lilt in her Midwestern accent I couldn't quite place, the fire in her voice — I was hooked.

I seized the opportunity to introduce myself to the recent Kansas transplant, proving that tornadoes could exist in the Big Apple, too. One whirlwind romance later, we were here: one week away from our picture-perfect Valentine's Day wedding.

And the wedding had to be perfect.

A perfect wedding commanded a perfect location, and I had pulled every influential string my father held to secure the Waldorf Astoria. As payback, my father had made it crystal clear that this new restaurant deal had to go off without a hitch.

If this deal fell apart, he wouldn't just be disappointed—he would make sure my spotless reputation took a very public hit.

I took a deep breath.

What was I worrying about?

Everything was going perfectly according to plan. The wedding. The restaurant. Our future.

And yet…

I reached for my jacket and hesitated. Would Annie be happy?

I had never doubted myself before—why start now? I had given her everything. Stability. Status. A future she'd never have had without me.

Hadn't I?

I clenched my jaw and threw on the coat. This was nothing. A crack in the veneer. Nothing I couldn't smooth over.

And yet—I could still hear my father's voice, clear as the clink of crystal in a five-star dining room. I was eight years old, standing on a stepstool in the family estate's gleaming kitchen, a trembling spoon in my hand.

"Again," my father had said, barely glancing at the ruined sauce. "You over-whisked the hollandaise. If it's not perfect, it's trash."

The hollandaise wasn't trash. I had tasted it—it was good. Not perfect, maybe, but good. But my father never tolerated good enough.

I had made the sauce twelve times that night until my arm ached and the last attempt met my father's impossible standards. And the next morning?

My father had thrown it out.

"No one wants day-old hollandaise, son. What matters is that you can do it again tomorrow."

The memory soured in my stomach as I reached for my keys. Perfection wasn't just expected—it was demanded.

And he couldn't afford even the smallest imperfection.

Not in the restaurant.

Not in the wedding.

Not in Annie.

Chapter Five

Annie

I tiptoed into Jordan's hospital room, gingerly closing the door behind me. One hand balanced a triple-packet sweetened coffee. Flaky crumbs of iced sugar showered my right hand, the thousand-calorie cruller crumbling by the second. The society page was tucked neatly beneath my arm. I tried to ignore the 24-point headline: *Parker Restaurant Heir Off the Menu!* The article below detailed the plans for the posh Waldorf reception, the extravagant European honeymoon, and my $11,000 Berta Baliti gown. I grimaced. After the breakfast in my hand, I might need two of those gowns to cover my backside. Carbs went to my hips in a New York minute.

"Can't be helped." I shrugged. My blood sugar had dropped dangerously low. The last thing I wanted to happen was to wind up in the bed with Jordan.

Sort of.

As I tried to latch the door without making

a sound, the cruller took a nosedive.

"Cheese and crackers!" I cursed. An unbidden giggle escaped me. I hadn't said that in years.

A muffled mumble sounded behind me. Jordan stirred in the hospital bed. I stared, holding my breath until I tinged the color of the blue walls. I hung back, silent as a church mouse, until the rhythmic rise and fall of his chest convinced me he remained asleep. The blip-beep of the pulse monitor kept time like a glowing green metronome. I returned my attention to the fallen doughnut.

"Five-second rule," I whispered. I bent down to retrieve the cruller. The roundness of my bottom pushed against the check of my chef pants. The pulse monitor ticked a beat or two faster.

"Gosh, what I wouldn't give to get a piece of that."

I shot to attention, the cruller forgotten. I whipped around and stared balefully at Jordan, now very much awake.

"Excuse me?" I demanded.

"The cruller! I meant the cruller!" Jordan defended. "I have had nothing that can't be squeezed through a tube since I got here." He gestured to the IV snaking into his arm.

I grinned sheepishly. "Yeah. I know. I came with you. In the ambulance. I mean, I arrived here because I rode you. With you! Oh, never mind!" I expelled two full cheeks worth of air. The fire in my cheeks was redder than my hair.

"You always did have a way with words. As I recall, the last ones you said to me still have Mayor Tucker's ears ringing."

"Yeah? Well, that blue ribbon was supposed to be mine." I glared at him. "It should have been mine."

Like a lot of things.

The years had treated Jordan well. Tiny laugh lines tugged at the corners of his generous mouth, belying his characteristic good humor. Even beneath the baggy hospital fashion statement, his muscles rippled — a telling hint of long hours working in the fields of his father's farm. Honest muscles. Earned from a hard day's work. Not in a mirror-filled gym where all you had to show for it afterward was how pretty you looked.

His honey-blonde hair could use a trim, though. It hung a little low over his hazel eyes. Looked like Fred Bean's old English sheepdog. A smirk snuck across my face as I absentmindedly wondered if Jordan's nose was cold. I shivered. I rubbed my arm with my free hand.

Why did they always keep hospitals so darn chilly?

Jordan looked all warm and cozy under his

blanket. I hesitated, then sat on the edge of the bed, tracing a finger along the spread. My finger hit something solid.

"Wow, that's hard," I stated. Jordan's eyes widened to the size of pie plates as I whipped back the covers. "The cast is completely set," I continued. "The doc says it'll have to stay on for a while. You banged your leg up pretty bad."

"Pretty bad? Now, there's an oxymoron for you," Jordan postulated. An impish twinkle developed in his eye as he shifted himself upright in the bed. "Speaking of oxymorons, I hear you're happily married now, Annie."

I bounded off the bed, bouncing Jordan's bum leg. He winced.

"I am not!" I countered, jamming both fists downward and stamping a petite foot. Jordan grinned through his pain. I rolled my eyes, realizing I'd taken Jordan's bait — hook, line, and sinker.

I paused for a moment, reconsidering. "What I meant to say was, I'm not married yet. But, when I *do* take my vows at the end of this week, I will be *most* happily married to a man I truly love, and intend to stay that way, forever and ever."

"Amen."

I folded my arms so close to my chest that my fingers blanched.

"Who's the lucky guy?" Jordan pressed.

"He's from a very important family. They have several restaurants here in the city."

"Hungry guy."

I leveled a sudden, accusing stare at Jordan, "Wait. How did you know I was getting married?"

Jordan smoothed the bed linens over his lap. "Did you know Granny McGowan makes great apple pie? I've grown to love apple pie. I could sit for *hours* over apple pie."

"Granny McGowan? *My* Granny McGowan?"

"Wonderful woman. Loves to talk. You wouldn't believe what Mrs. Murphy's daughter is up to. When I think of what she has put that poor woman through—my heart just goes out to her." He raised a hand to his chest, and he lowered his head.

"All right, Dr. Phil. Fess up. You've been checking up on me." I waggled a finger at him. He feigned shock.

"Whatever gave you that idea?"

"I've had Granny McGowan's apple pie."

An awkward silence filled the room. Jordan broke ranks first. "She worries about you, you know."

"Apparently, she's not the only one."

"You never gave me a chance to explain.

After the contest, you packed your bags and just took off. No one knew where you were going—what you were doing."

"That's just it, Jordan. I *did* know where I was going. I knew *exactly* what I wanted to do. And you took that opportunity away from me."

Jordan started to speak, but he seemed to get hung up on the words. He stopped, then tried again. "Look, it doesn't really matter how we ended things. You will always have a special place in my heart. So, yeah, I'm going to worry about you, too. New York's a big town. Anything could happen."

"Yeah, like you could wreck your car and break your leg."

Jordan shrugged. "Bones heal."

Hearts not so much.

"What were you doing in front of my restaurant, anyway? Did Granny send you to check up on me?"

"That was *your* restaurant?"

"Not exactly *my* restaurant. It belongs to a friend. It's been in his family for generations."

"Your fiancé's place?"

I rocked my head. "No, no, no. A wonderful old man named Louie. He took me in when I came to New York." A frown drew the corners of my mouth down.

"What's the matter?" Jordan asked.

"Nothing."

"Nothing doesn't make you look like Sheriff Lubbock's Basset Hound back home."

Dogs were big back in Kansas.

"What's up?" he continued.

I squinted at Jordan. He could be such a weenie. He definitely had some latent weenie tendencies. But you couldn't argue that he'd always been a good listener. I took a deep breath.

"Louie's going to lose the restaurant. Business has been a little slow lately, and he's behind on the mortgage payments. If he can't come up with a balloon payment, he's got to close the doors. I've been trying to figure out a way to help him, but all I keep coming up with is goose eggs. I hardly make enough to pay my own bills. My fiancé's family is even paying for the wedding."

"Can't he help you out?" Jordan suggested.

"He doesn't even want me working there. I think the only reason he doesn't have me dressed in a tight white skirt chasing a fuzzy yellow ball at 'The Club' is that his father has 'big plans' for me as head chef at his fancy new restaurant."

"I'm confused. Isn't that what you always wanted?"

"I guess."

But was it?

I used to know exactly what I wanted—my

34

own kitchen, my own rules, my own legacy. Now, everything felt like someone else's plan, and I was just along for the ride.

"Is that your final answer?"

"Hah, hah. Look, Vitello's may not be perfect. It drives me insane when I need shitake mushrooms, and all I have is Portobellos. But it's family. Louie and Curtis."

"Curtis?"

"Our jack-of-all-trades. You met him. He rescued your hotdog."

"Someone needs to give that man a medal. But seriously. That was a human being? I thought I'd run into a building."

"Nope. Just a hydrant. Speaking of which, you never answered my question. Why are you here?"

"Um," Jordan began, his eyes darting around the room. "It's like you said. I had some business in town and Granny found out. So, she just asked me to check in on you while I was here."

"Business? What business?"

Jordan's eyes flickered for a moment before he forced a grin. "Like I said, just business." But his fingers fidgeted with the edge of the blanket, a habit I remembered seeing whenever he was hiding something. "It's nothing."

"Answer me!" I smacked the bed,

accidentally smacking Jordan's leg simultaneously. He clamped his teeth together, creating an exaggerated, if awkward, smile.

The wide room door swung open. A large woman in pink scrubs entered, eyes scanning the clipboard in her hand.

"Ah! I see we're feeling better," the nurse commented. She reached for the blood pressure cuff hanging around her neck.

"Oh, I'm feeling," Jordan forced through clenched teeth. "But I don't know that 'better' would be the word I'd use."

The nurse checked Jordan's vitals, nodding and clucking at regular intervals. "Well, young man, Doc's got me administering some painkillers and then he's releasing you, but he wants your pretty little wife here to keep a close eye on you."

Jordan and I shook our heads in tandem.

"She's not my wife," Jordan hastily interjected.

"No? Then you may want her to leave the room. I have to uncover your backside to administer this shot. Works better in a large muscle group."

I grinned from ear to ear. I patted Jordan's free hand. "Oh, sweetheart. I couldn't possibly leave you alone. Not when you're in so much pain. What he meant to say, ma'am, is I'm not his wife yet." I wiggled the finger with my engagement ring. "We're engaged. Go ahead. Give him the shot. I'll stay."

A little white lie, but so worth it.

"Okay, then," the nurse agreed.

And before Jordan could protest, the needle was in his rump.

Chapter Six

Trent

"Annie's in the hospital? When? How did this happen?" I blustered as I paced through Vitello's kitchen. My Ferragamo loafer slid on a greasy tile and I nearly went down. "Jesus! What a dump!" I bellowed as I caught myself on the counter.

The counters were cluttered, the walls stained, and the fluorescent light flickered like it might give up any second. To me, it was chaos—a kitchen on life support. But Louie wiped the stove like it was an altar, his hands moving with a reverence I couldn't understand. For a second, I almost envied him.

Some customers in the restaurant cast anxious glances my way. A few shawl-draped *nonnas* exchanged whispers in hurried Italian.

Pah! What did I care?

One old man casually reached up, turned off his hearing aid, and resumed an enthusiastic slurping of his minestrone.

Blech!

Louie opened his mouth to explain. I guillotined the attempt. "We were supposed to meet the banquet coordinator in a half hour. If we don't decide between the foie gras and the shrimp, it will be a catastrophe. What am I supposed to do? God, I've got such a headache!"

For a split second, I thought about Annie lying in that hospital bed. What if she'd been seriously hurt? But then my stomach tightened at the thought of how it would unravel everything — the wedding, the restaurant deal, my father's expectations.

I wanted to believe it was just the stress of planning, the pressure of keeping my father happy, and Annie's stubborn attachment to this crumbling relic of a restaurant. But a tiny voice I'd been ignoring for weeks whispered something else — that maybe Annie wasn't just clinging to Vitello's. Maybe she was clinging to a life that didn't include me. I shoved the thought aside. There was no time for worst-case scenarios.

Curtis mumbled under his breath. "I'd like to mash *that* shrimp into foie gras right about now."

Curtis's jaw tightened, his eyes narrowing at me with an intensity that sent an unexpected flicker of unease up my spine. He didn't just look annoyed — he looked like he was deciding I wasn't worth the dirt on his boots. I brushed it off. What did I care what a glorified janitor thought? I shot him a look.

Louie patted the big man's back. "It's okay, Curtis. The young man is only acting crazy because he is concerned."

Louie wiped his hands on a dishtowel, his movements slow. He glanced at the floor for a moment before answering, his tone overly polite.

"Sì, he is only worried," he reiterated, but there was a hesitation in his voice, a pointed calm that felt like it was meant to cut.

Was that a dig? From him? I didn't like it one bit.

Curtis dredged an eggplant filet through flour. Eggplant beignets were today's featured appetizer, if you believed the chalkboard sign out on the sidewalk. I gagged. Eggplants? In beignets?

No wonder this place was dying.

"Worried about his damned deposit, I'll bet," Curtis growled.

I took a step back as the large man advanced toward me. He shook a floured finger in my face. "Why don't you take that fancy toy you've got on your hip and just make a damned phone call?"

"No, no, no. Rescheduling is out. What with the wedding just around the corner, and it being on Valentine's Day. It's chaotic enough as it is."

I cared about Annie, but timing was everything. The wedding wasn't just about us — it was about the Parker name. Annie would understand that. She always understood what needed to come first, even if she didn't always like it.

"We've already pulled a zillion strings to make this happen as it is." I paused my frenetic pace and calculated things in my head.

"The hospital's only five minutes away. I can swing by, pick Annie up and, if we're lucky enough to avoid cross-town traffic, we might still make the appointment."

My father would lose his mind if I messed this up. The wedding was more than a personal milestone. It was the perfect PR opportunity for the Parker brand. And Vitello's? This place wasn't even on the same playing field. Annie had to see that.

"Maybe the nice hospital people can give you something for your headache," Louie suggested.

As I headed for the door, I didn't miss Curtis' last parry.

"Yeah. Like a lobotomy."

I yanked open the door, but before stepping out, I glimpsed Louie's tired eyes watching me. For a moment, I hesitated, something unspoken hanging in the air. It wasn't guilt—I didn't owe these people anything. But as I left, I couldn't shake the feeling that maybe, just maybe, Annie saw something in them I'd been too blind to notice.

Chapter Seven

Annie

I pulled the blanket up over Jordan's broad chest as we sat in the backseat of Louie's '67 Cadillac. He had howled like a baby when the needle pierced the skin. But now he slept like a log. I brushed a lock of hair from his closed eyes. He looked so peaceful. Handsome. Like someone you could easily fall in love with.

Hard to believe after the last time we were together.

It had been five years ago at the Kansas State Fair. I entered the casserole competition, the Queen Mother of all the cooking events at the fair. My recipe was a shoo-in, the favorite to win.

Southwest Chicken Acapulco.

Some south-of-the-border zest for the fine folks of the Midwest. I had pitched the concept to Jordan one night while we created a little of our own spice south of the border in the hayloft at Jordan's family farm.

"With this prize money, maybe I can finally

open my own restaurant," I bubbled eagerly.

"First, you gotta win," Jordan teased.

I grinned and punched him in the arm. "Are you kidding? With you backing me up, there's nothing I can't do!"

As the two of us tumbled in the sweet-smelling hay, he listened as I concocted my tantalizing list of ingredients for this recipe. His warm, sensual kisses brought me from a slow simmer to a downright sizzle.

The next day, however, I boiled over when Jordan entered the same contest the day of the fair with a near-identical recipe and whisked the blue ribbon right out from under my nose. Believe you me, I served up a tasty response by unloading the rest of my Southwest Chicken Acapulco on his head and putting miles of yellow brick road between me and my traitorous, now ex-boyfriend.

I couldn't believe he was here, right in front of me again, my personal flying monkey in the Emerald City I'd found. And only days before my wedding to Trent. I sighed. Where was Glinda when you really needed her?

Or a well-placed house?

"You sure you know what you're doing, Annie?" Curtis asked from the driver's seat. He adjusted the rearview of the Coupe de Ville to reflect his concerned look. I sat behind him on the passenger side of the bench backseat, Jordan's snoring head cradled in my lap.

The doctor had released Jordan but warned he would need help to get around and get dressed. He would also likely need someone to give him a sponge bath.

I had left that part out when I recruited Curtis to help me transport Jordan to my apartment.

"What was I supposed to do, Curtis? He's from out of town. He doesn't know anybody else here, and he needs help."

"Needs driving lessons is what he needs," Curtis mumbled, but had agreed to help me out. The Cadillac bumped over one of New York's signature potholes. I winced as I gingerly steadied Jordan's head. I tucked in the loose edges of the blanket. Curtis saw it all in the rearview. He grinned at me. I stuck out my tongue.

Truth was, I had absolutely no idea what I was doing. But it was too late now. He wasn't a pair of shoes I'd bought at Bloomingdale's. I couldn't return him for store credit.

I had taken him out of the hospital and now I was stuck with him.

With Curtis' help, I muscled Jordan up the stairs to my three-story walk-up. I smiled sheepishly at Mrs. Katz on two as we passed the older woman on the landing. She stared at Jordan flopped over Curtis' shoulders like a sack of potatoes.

"Afternoon, Mrs. Katz. Looks like it's going to be a beautiful Valentine's Day, doesn't it?"

The blue-haired septuagenarian eyeballed us. I suppose the sight of a large African American man and a young woman hauling an unconscious young man in a hospital gown was a little unusual—even for New York.

Ugh, I wished Jordan's clothes hadn't been destroyed. The hospital staff had needed to cut them off to tend to his injuries. And the rest of his clothes had been ruined in the accident, soaked by the spewing water of the fire hydrant.

Hospital chic it is.

As I struggled to close the back of Jordan's gown against Mrs. Katz's fine sensibilities, I realized I needn't have bothered. I'm pretty sure I caught a peek of her dentures through a discreet smile. I suppressed a grin.

Jordan always did have a nice derrière.

Two deadbolts later, we had settled Jordan on the Murphy bed. Curtis gave me a great big bear hug.

"You be careful, now, you hear? And don't do anything I wouldn't do." He kissed my cheek.

I smiled. "That doesn't leave much, you know."

The big man chuckled deeply and departed, leaving me alone with my new houseguest. I shrugged off my purse and deposited it on the kitchen counter. When I pulled out my cell phone, my eyes popped wide.

Fifteen missed calls and messages!

I brought a hesitant finger to the screen and tapped. Trent's blustering voice squawked from the tiny speaker.

"Annie! Where are you?" I could hear his blood pressure rising through the phone. "We had an appointment with the Waldorf people and I was informed you were at the hospital. Of course, that idiot of a sous chef told me the *wrong* hospital, so of course you weren't there when I arrived. We need to talk. I have a meeting with Dad first, but I'll stop by your place later."

The Waldorf meeting!

How could I have forgotten?

I looked at my snoring ex-boyfriend on the bed—my bed.

Oh, yeah. That's how I forgot.

That was also why Trent could *not* come by my place! The other fourteen messages were variations on the same theme. I needed to figure this out—now.

I scrambled to my bathroom and gathered a few toiletries and a white, fluffy towel. If I had to give Jordan a sponge bath, I'd rather do it now while he was passed out on pain meds.

And before Trent showed up.

I dug through my chest of drawers, figuring some of Trent's old clothes would fit him. I'd probably have to cut the leg to accommodate the cast. Trent would not be pleased.

"What the hey? In for a penny, in for a pound." I sat gently on the edge of the bed. Jordan didn't stir. I inhaled deeply. "Here goes nothing."

Gently, I tucked the blankets discreetly around his body and worked his arms from the hospital gown sleeves. I dropped it on the floor behind me. When I turned, my breath caught in my throat.

I'd forgotten how beautiful he was.

I grabbed blindly for the washcloth in the basin, the warm water barely comparable to the warmth I suddenly felt surging through my veins. Michelangelo himself would have marveled at the ripple of muscle beneath Jordan's sun-kissed skin. I drew the washcloth evenly along the curve of his bicep and down his sinewy forearm before dipping the cloth into the water, swishing and wringing it.

I brushed the warm, soapy cloth under his chiseled jawline, pausing briefly over the delicate hollow of his neck. The strong, steady beat of his heart pulsed through the cloth. I squeezed the washcloth over his chest, rivulets of water running over his pectorals, and followed down along his abdomen.

"Annie."

My heart leaped into my throat. The washcloth plopped into the water. Soapy bubbles and water splashed everywhere. One hand flew to cover the sharp gasp from my mouth, the other to my eyes to shield me from—well—you know.

I waited, my heart thrumming in my veins—waited for him to say something. But all I got was a big, fat, rattling snore.

I peeked through my fingers. Jordan tossed his head, but he did not wake. He'd just been talking in his sleep.

"What am I doing?" I finally muttered. "There's a naked man in my bed. I'm about to be married, and I have a naked man in my bed."

My phone buzzed.

Trent!

My eyes wandered back to Jordan.

"I am in so much trouble," I groaned. Jordan's groan succeeded my own. Frantically, I fumbled to put the hospital gown back on him.

"Have to tell her. Need to tell Annie," Jordan mumbled from his drug-induced stupor.

"Have to tell Annie what? That she's nuts? Way ahead of you, pal," I quipped. I got his first arm through a sleeve.

Just then, the door buzzer sounded. I froze as Trent's voice filtered through the intercom.

"Annie, it's Trent. Buzz me in. We need to

talk."

I laughed maniacally as I pulled Jordan's other arm through the second sleeve. "Oh, yes. We definitely need to talk. Please, sit down. I'll make some tea. Pay no attention to the half-dressed man in my bed."

If Trent saw Jordan here, it wouldn't just ruin the wedding—it would destroy everything I'd worked so hard to build. Trent wouldn't understand, and honestly, I wasn't sure I could explain it to myself.

"Gotta let her know," Jordan continued his unconscious rambling.

"Let me know what? Good lord!" I grunted under Jordan's weight as I struggled to sit him upright.

"Annie?" Trent called again. "Oh, thank you, Mrs. Katz. Yes, I'm going up to see Annie. Thank you for letting me in."

I froze. The intercom fell silent.

"Mrs. Katz! Why did you let him in? Don't you know this is New York? Nobody is nice to anybody!"

Trent's footsteps echoed up the stairwell. I redoubled my efforts.

"Bought a ring," Jordan whispered.

I stopped cold. "What?"

"The contest. Didn't want her to *lose*," he mumbled. "Wanted to *marry* her."

The words landed like a cast-iron skillet to the head. My throat tightened, a hundred unspoken questions vying for attention.

What did he mean? Why now? Why, after all these years?

I dropped Jordan's head onto the pillow, where he emitted a loud, rattling snore.

Chapter Eight

Jordan

I was pinned—or at least it felt like I was. My body was heavy, weighed down by some invisible force, making it impossible to move. My head pounded, and there was a dull ache somewhere behind my eyes. I tried to open them, but everything felt sticky and thick, like I was swimming through syrup.

Lavender. Was that lavender?

I groaned, my throat raw, as I tried to shift. Pain shot through my leg, sharp and blinding. Oh, right. The cast. I winced, the ache in my leg quickly pulling me back to reality. The accident. The hospital. Annie.

Where was I?

Something tugged at my arm, and I tried to blink away the fog. My head lolled to the side. I could just make out the blurry shape of someone leaning over me, pulling at me with frantic hands. The soft scent of lavender clung to the air, familiar and oddly comforting. It was enough to wake me up just a little more.

"Jordan, get up!" the voice hissed, muffled like it was coming through water.

Annie.

Another sharp tug, and my eyes fluttered open, blurry shapes slowly coming into focus. Annie knelt beside me, yanking at my arm with an urgency that made no sense to my sleep-addled brain.

"Annie?" I croaked, my voice rough, throat dry as sandpaper.

"Shhh!" she whispered, her eyes wide and panicked. "Jordan, you need to get up now. Trent's here!"

Trent.

The fog in my brain lifted. Thoughts of Annie and Trent together filled the cracks, bringing a fresh wave of discomfort. I'd been around long enough—and eaten enough of Granny McGowan's pie—to know what this moment meant. Trent wasn't just her fiancé—he was probably the type of guy who would see my presence here as something far worse than a misunderstanding.

Another loud knock echoed from the door, and my heart stuttered.

"Annie? You in there?" Trent's voice boomed through the apartment.

Oh, crap.

That cleared the rest of the cobwebs from

my brain.

"Jordan, if Trent sees you like this, I'm dead," Annie said, her hands still tugging at me. "I need to hide you. Now."

I tried to sit up, my limbs heavy and uncooperative. Pain radiated from my leg, the cast dragging awkwardly across the bed.

"Annie," I slurred, confusion still thick in my voice. "What's going on?"

She glanced toward the door again, panic etched into every line of her face. "Jordan, please. Just move!"

I swore under my breath, wincing as I tried to swing my legs off the bed. The cast hit the floor with a dull thud, a stark reminder of my limited mobility. "I can't exactly run out of here," I muttered. "But I'm moving."

"Not fast enough," she hissed, looping her arm through mine and practically dragging me toward the sliding glass door that led to the balcony.

The February air hit me like an ice bath, the thin hospital gown no match for the wind. The cast thumped against the balcony, a frigid anchor keeping me teetering on the edge.

"Stay out here and stay quiet!" Annie whispered sharply, her face pale as she drew the curtains shut behind me.

I was freezing. The wind cut through the

gown like it wasn't even there, and I wrapped my arms around myself, shivering violently. My toes were already numb, and the ache in my leg pulsed harder in the cold.

Inside, muffled voices reached my ears—Trent's deep and smooth, Annie's bright and unnaturally cheerful. I caught fragments of what they were saying, but the wind howled louder, drowning out most of their words.

This was a disaster. I had a cast on my leg, was freezing to death, and was now stuck on a balcony while my ex-girlfriend tried to keep her fiancé from finding me.

I leaned against the railing, my brain sluggish from the medicine. Across the street, two older women stood at their window, staring at me with wide, delighted eyes. One pointed, and the other's grin spread so wide I could almost hear her laughing.

The wind caught my gown, and I grabbed at the fabric too late. Their shocked expressions were burned into my brain as I turned my back, cursing under my breath.

I couldn't stay out here much longer. My body shook uncontrollably. I wasn't sure if it was from the cold or the ridiculousness of the situation. I knocked again on the glass door, hoping Annie would have mercy. No answer.

"Rats!" I heard Annie's voice through the

door. "It's just rats in the walls! You know how these old buildings are."

Rats? Really?

I glanced at the fire escape and the bathroom window over it. It wasn't a good idea, but it was the only idea I had.

With a deep breath, I clambered over the railing. The metal was slippery under my bare feet. The cast dragged awkwardly with every step. My fingers were stiff, but I fumbled the bathroom window open and half-fell inside.

I hit the tile with a loud thud, my cast landing with a clunk that echoed through the space.

"Oh, that noise?" Annie's voice floated through the bathroom door, chipper and quick. "Just the old pipes! Terrible plumbing in these buildings."

I groaned, leaning against the sink to catch my breath. My reflection in the mirror was a sight — plaster cast, hair sticking out at odd angles, hospital gown barely hanging on.

Finally, the front door clicked shut, and Annie rushed into the bathroom, her face flushed.

"Are you okay?" she whispered, her voice frantic but soft.

I blinked at her, still shivering. "Annie," I said, my voice hoarse, "you owe me so big for this."

Her laugh was nervous but genuine, her hand fluttering to her mouth. "Yeah, I know. Come on. Let's get you warm."

She helped me limp to the couch, her arm steadying me as I dragged the cast across the floor.

When I finally collapsed onto the cushions, I sighed, my head spinning and my body trembling. Despite the absurdity of the last few minutes—despite the cold, the pain, and the humiliation—there was something grounding about being here, about Annie fussing over me.

For a moment, it felt like the old days, before everything went sideways.

"Jordan, I'm really sorry," she said, tucking a blanket around me.

I shook my head, a faint smile tugging at my lips. "It's fine, Annie. This..." I gestured vaguely at the room. "This is nothing new for us, right?"

Her smile faltered for a second, and I caught the flicker of something in her eyes.

Even if it was a disaster, there was nowhere else I'd rather be.

Chapter Nine

Annie

The door clicked shut behind Trent, and the silence that followed felt like a weight had been lifted from the apartment. I stood frozen for a moment, listening to the muffled sound of his footsteps fading down the hallway. My heart, which had been hammering in my chest the entire time, finally settled into something resembling a normal rhythm.

Thank God.

That had been way too close.

I leaned against the back of the couch, running a hand through my hair as I let out a long, shaky breath. The whole time Trent had been here, I'd been bracing myself for him to figure out that something was off—for him to hear a noise I couldn't explain, or worse, glimpse Jordan skulking around in his hospital gown. But somehow, I'd gotten through the conversation without raising too many red flags.

I pushed myself off the couch and headed

toward the bathroom. It had sounded like the big dummy had climbed through the window.

I grinned wryly. I guess I couldn't blame him. He'd been out on the balcony long enough to freeze his ass off, and after everything we'd just been through, I owed him a little warmth.

"Jordan," I whispered as I opened the bathroom door. He was slumped in a heap on the tile floor, his arms wrapped tightly around himself, shivering violently. His hair was a wild mess, and his hospital gown was barely hanging on. He looked like he'd been through hell.

"Are you okay?"

I blinked at her, still shivering. "Annie," I said, my voice hoarse, "you owe me so big for this."

We exchanged a few more words on the way to the couch, including an apology for exposing him to the elements.

He blinked up at me, his teeth still chattering. "You know, you could have just told Trent I was the maid. I'm sure he would've believed it."

I snorted, grabbing his arm to steady him. "Oh, sure. Nope. This was the only way. Believe me, Trent's is not the type of guy who's fine with his fiancée hiding her ex-boyfriend in her apartment."

"Okay, fair point," he muttered. "But next

59

time, maybe don't stick me outside in a hospital gown in the middle of February."

I couldn't help but laugh, despite the awkwardness of the situation. "Noted."

Once Jordan was settled on the couch, I grabbed a blanket from the armchair and tossed it over him. He looked a little better now that he was out of the cold, but I could still see the exhaustion in his eyes, the lingering effects of the accident weighing him down.

"Get some rest," I said softly. "You can borrow some of Trent's clothes while I dry yours."

He nodded weakly, leaning back against the cushions, and I made my way toward the bag of his wet clothes that I'd dumped on the floor earlier. They were soaked from the fire hydrant, and I wrinkled my nose as I picked up the duffel. It was heavy with moisture, and something slid out of it, landing on the floor with a soggy thud.

I frowned, bending down to retrieve it. It was a crumpled piece of paper, damp and smudged, but still legible. I smoothed it out with my fingers, trying to make sense of what I was looking at.

Whisk It All: The Ultimate Culinary Showdown

My eyes widened as I scanned the words. It was an application form for the Whisk It All competition, the most prestigious cooking competition in the country. I knew all about it. Every chef did. Only a certain number of entrants were allowed each year. The winner walked away with enough prestige to boost their career to the next level.

But the cash prize…that's what caught my attention.

I sat down on the floor, my heart pounding again, but for a completely different reason this time.

The prize money was $50,000.

That was almost enough to cover the funds Louie needed for the restaurant. I felt a spark of hope flare to life in my chest, but I squashed it down almost immediately. This was Jordan's application. I couldn't just…

But then my eyes drifted back to the number on the page.

Fifty thousand dollars.

I closed my eyes, the weight of everything pressing down on me all at once. Vitello's was more than just a restaurant. It was Louie's life, his legacy, and if I didn't find a way to save it, the place would be gone. It wasn't just a building—it was a part of who I was.

It was family.

Louie didn't have the money to save it, and neither did I. The bank was ready to swoop in and take the restaurant away from us. And I couldn't bear to let that happen.

But this competition…this could be the answer. The prize money would solve everything.

I glanced over at Jordan, who was already half-asleep on the couch, his chest rising and falling in slow, steady breaths. He looked so peaceful, so oblivious that I was staring down at his application like some sort of forbidden treasure.

I bit my lip, the guilt gnawing at the edges of my thoughts.

Could I really do this? Could I really take his spot in the competition?

I swallowed hard, the lump in my throat making it difficult to think clearly. The rational side of me whispered 'no', telling me it was wrong. But the desperate part of me — the part that was watching Louie's dream slip away — was screaming 'yes'.

I could save Vitello's. I could make everything right.

I stared at the soggy application in my hand, my mind spinning with a thousand thoughts at once. Maybe Jordan wouldn't even notice. After all, he wasn't in any shape to compete right now. I could take his place, win the prize money, and explain everything to him later. He'd understand…right?

He had to.

I glanced at the application again, my heart pounding in my chest. This was my chance. My only chance.

I didn't have time to waste. The competition deadline was fast approaching, and I couldn't afford to wait for Jordan to wake up and have a conversation about it. I had to act now.

I grabbed my phone and took a deep breath, quickly typing the competition's website and pulling up the application form. My hands shook as I filled out the required fields, using Jordan's information where necessary. Name, address, credentials — everything I needed was right there in front of me, thanks to the soggy application in my hand.

I hesitated when I reached the last step — the submit button. My thumb hovered over it for a second, and the guilt surged up again, twisting my stomach into knots.

What if Jordan found out? What if he didn't understand? What if he was mad?

But then I thought of Louie, sitting in his office, the weight of the world on his shoulders, knowing that his restaurant was slipping through his fingers.

And I thought of Trent, his voice in my ear, always reminding me that places like Vitello's were no longer relevant and should be allowed to die out.

"Natural selection," he'd suggested.

I couldn't let that happen. I wouldn't.

With one final, shaky breath, I hit submit.

The screen blinked, and a confirmation message appeared. My heart lurched in my chest, and I stared at the screen, my pulse racing. It was done. I had submitted the application. I was officially in the competition.

A mixture of relief and dread washed over me as I set my phone down on the coffee table. The relief came from knowing that I had a shot—a real shot—at saving Vitello's. But the dread…that was from the guilt. I had just taken Jordan's shot at fame and fortune, and I knew there was no easy way to explain that if—or when—he found out.

Hey, turnabout is fair play.

At least, that was the reasoning I was arguing in my head. I glanced over at him again. He was still fast asleep, completely unaware of what I'd just done. Part of me wanted to wake him up, to come clean and tell him everything, but the other part of me—the desperate part—knew that I couldn't risk it. Not yet.

I needed to win first. Then, maybe, I could explain.

But until then, I'd have to keep this a secret. And that meant keeping Jordan in the dark, at least for now.

I got up from the floor, my legs feeling shaky, and grabbed a towel from the bathroom. Jordan's clothes were still a soggy mess on the floor, and I figured the least I could do was try to dry them out a little. After all, I owed him that much after everything I'd just put him through.

As I wrung out his clothes, my mind kept drifting back to the competition. Whisk It All was no joke. The best chefs in the country competed in it, and the challenges were designed to push every competitor to their limit. Winning it wouldn't be easy. I'd have to be at the top of my game.

But I wasn't just doing this for myself. I was doing it for Louie. For Vitello's.

The guilt still gnawed at me, but I pushed it aside. I didn't have time to dwell on it. The competition was my only chance, and I couldn't let that slip away.

I folded Jordan's now slightly less-damp clothes and draped them over the radiator, then took a seat on the couch beside him. He stirred slightly, his eyelids fluttering but not quite opening.

There were faint dark circles under his eyes. He looked exhausted, and it made the guilt flare up again, more insistent this time.

I reached for the blanket and tucked it around him a little more snugly, my fingers brushing against his arm. He didn't react, too far gone in whatever dreamland his brain danced in.

I sat back, pulling my knees up to my chest and resting my chin on top of them. I stared at the coffee table, my thoughts racing.

Had I done the right thing?

Part of me wanted to believe that I had, that this was just a means to an end. Vitello's needed saving.

But another part of me—the part that was nagging at my conscience—told me I'd crossed a line.

I sighed, rubbing my temples. There was no going back now. I'd made my choice, and I'd have to live with it. I just hoped that when the time came, I'd be able to explain it all to Jordan in a way that made sense.

I didn't want to hurt him. But right now, I didn't have a choice.

I glanced at my phone, checking the time. There were only a few days left until the competition started, and I needed to prepare. I had no idea what challenges I'd be facing, but I knew they'd be tough. I'd have to be even tougher if I wanted to come out on top.

And I had to win. There was no other option.

As I stood up, I took one last look at Jordan before heading toward the kitchen. I needed to plan my strategy, and that meant getting my head in the game. I couldn't afford to let guilt or fear hold me back.

For now, I had to focus. I had to win. For Louie. For Vitello's.

And maybe...for me, too.

Chapter Ten

Trent

As I walked down the narrow hallway of Annie's apartment building, something gnawed at me, like a memory just out of reach, teasing and elusive. The hallway smelled faintly of musty wood and cheap cleaner, the faint hum of a radiator echoing against the scuffed walls. My footsteps seemed too loud in the quiet, as if the building itself were holding its breath. My fingers drummed against my phone, the rhythm fast and sharp, mirroring the unease twisting in my gut.

Annie was acting strange.

She hadn't been herself lately, but today? Today had been particularly bizarre. The nervous laughs, the way her eyes kept darting toward the balcony. And then there was the excuse about rats in the walls.

Rats? I'd been coming over to her apartment for years, and not once had I heard anything close to the clunks and thuds that echoed through her walls today.

It didn't sit right. Annie didn't rattle

easily—she was steady, practical, grounded. But this? This was something else entirely.

My footsteps slowed as I stepped outside. I stopped just in front of the building, staring blankly at the sidewalk.

What was she hiding?

I looked up toward her apartment and was surprised to see the bathroom curtains fluttering out the open window.

Open window? In February?

I slipped my phone into my jacket pocket and crossed my arms, trying to shake off the feeling. Annie wasn't one to lie—not outright, at least—but something about her behavior was...off. And not just today. Over the past few weeks, she'd been distracted. Distant. Her mind wasn't on the wedding.

It was somewhere else.

And the more I thought about it, the more certain I became. Annie was keeping something from me.

But what?

If I was honest, I was keeping something from her, too.

I sighed, running a hand through my hair as I shoved my hands into my coat pockets. The Parker conglomerate had been working on this for months, quietly biding our time, waiting for Louie to fail. A balloon payment on Vitello's was due any day now, and everyone knew Louie didn't have the money to cover it. The second he missed it, the bank would swoop in, and that would be our chance. My father had been crystal clear on that.

Vitello's would be ours.

I rolled my shoulders, trying to ease the tension that built as I thought about it. It was just business, after all. The restaurant wasn't making money.

It was hemorrhaging it.

Louie had been sinking for years, and his stubborn refusal to sell out wasn't doing anyone any favors. But once Parker Enterprises had control, we'd bulldoze that rat trap and replace it with something worthwhile. Something Annie could be proud of. A gleaming, state-of-the-art restaurant, backed by the resources of a powerful conglomerate. It would be the crown jewel in the Parker empire.

I let out a slow breath, my lips curling into a small smile as I pictured it. Annie would get over Vitello's. Sure, she had a sentimental attachment to the place, but she wasn't unreasonable. Once she saw the vision, saw what we had planned, she'd embrace it.

How could she not?

I could see her there, in the kitchen, surrounded by an army of crisp sous chefs, shining pots and pans hanging from gleaming racks. No more cramped, outdated kitchen. No more broken-down appliances or faded countertops. No more struggling to keep the lights on.

It wasn't just about Louie or the restaurant. It was about Annie's refusal to let go of the past, her insistence on holding onto something that had already crumbled.

But then again, wasn't that part of what I loved about her? That fire, that stubbornness?

I could still remember the night she stayed at Vitello's until three in the morning, scrubbing the grease-stained stovetops after a busted fryer had dumped oil everywhere. Louie had waved her off, told her to go home, but she wouldn't leave until the kitchen was spotless.

"This place deserves better," she'd said, her voice fierce, her eyes blazing.

That was Annie—unyielding when something mattered to her.

A flicker of doubt nagged at me.

Would she see it that way?

Sure, she'd have everything she'd ever wanted—success, recognition, a legacy of her own. But I couldn't ignore the gnawing thought that maybe she'd see it as a betrayal.

I shook my head, trying to dismiss the unease. Annie loved me. She trusted me.

And in the end, she'd understand that this was for her. For us.

She had to.

But lately… lately, I wasn't so sure. She was getting antsy. More attached to Vitello's. More defensive about Louie. The last thing I needed was for her to snoop around or ask too many questions.

If she found out about the plan before the deal went through, it could ruin everything.

My thoughts flicked back to her behavior today—the tight smiles, the forced cheerfulness. The way she couldn't seem to meet my eyes.

She wasn't just hiding something.

She was scared.

The realization hit me like a bucket of ice water, and I stopped in my tracks, the city buzzing around me as I stood frozen on the sidewalk.

If Annie had figured out what the Parkers were planning for Vitello's, it wasn't just the deal that was at risk.

It was the wedding. Our future.

Everything.

I clenched my jaw, my fingers curling into fists inside my coat pockets.

She couldn't find out.

I'd worked too hard, invested too much in this. It was the perfect opportunity for her, for us. All I had to do was keep her focused on the wedding.

If I could keep her looking forward, keep her focused on the future we were building together, maybe she wouldn't look too closely at what was happening in the background.

But a small, insistent voice in the back of my mind whispered that it would not be that easy.

Annie wasn't stupid. She was passionate, stubborn, and fiercely loyal. If she even suspected that I was working against Louie, she'd dig until she found the truth.

And if she did…

What would she do if she found out?

I exhaled sharply, raking a hand through my hair. It didn't matter.

Once the deal went through, none of it would matter.

And Annie? She'd come around. She loved me.

And in the end, that was all that counted.

My phone buzzed.

I pulled it from my pocket, glancing at the name flashing on the screen. Charles Parker.

I hesitated before answering.

"Dad," I said, careful to keep my voice neutral.

"Trent." My father's voice was smooth, controlled. The voice of a man who never wasted words. "I'm coming into town earlier than planned."

I frowned, shifting my stance. "For the restaurant deal?"

A pause. A second too long.

"Among other things."

My grip tightened on the phone. My father never deviated from a plan. Not unless there was something more important.

"What other things?" I asked carefully.

Another pause. A long inhale, like he was debating how much to tell me.

"Just remember, son," he finally said, voice cooling. "Reputation is everything."

The line went dead.

I stared at my screen for a moment before shoving my phone back into my pocket, tension coiling in my chest.

Reputation is everything.

He had been saying that since I was a kid, drilling it into my head like a mantra. Like a warning.

But why say it now?

And what the hell was he really flying in for?

Chapter Eleven

Annie

The first night Jordan stayed over had been a disaster. I'd spent an hour trying to figure out how to fit both of us into my tiny apartment without things getting weird, and spoiler alert — it got weird.

My apartment only had one bed. A full-sized bed, which was already small for me. There was also the loveseat, but that thing was barely big enough for a hobbit, let alone a grown woman trying to avoid her ex-boyfriend's body heat.

I had insisted on the loveseat. "You take the bed," I'd said, dragging a blanket and pillow over to the small couch and trying not to look as awkward as I felt. "You're the one with the broken leg."

Jordan, of course, had argued. "Annie, I'm not going to let you sleep on that tiny thing. Just sleep in the bed."

"Nope, I'm fine," I had lied, arranging myself into what I could only describe as the fetal position of despair on the loveseat.

I'd been lying on the loveseat for what felt like an eternity, trying to ignore the sharp, lumpy cushions digging into my ribs. My legs dangled off the edge, my lower back was screaming, and the scratchy blanket barely covered my body. Every time I tried to shift, the loveseat would creak loudly, like it was mocking my determination to make this work.

But it wasn't working. I wasn't comfortable, and the longer I lay there, the more I could feel my body slowly locking up, every muscle tightening into knots.

I squeezed my eyes shut, trying to block out the quiet sounds of Jordan breathing from across the room. The bed.

My bed.

Where he was, no doubt, sprawled out comfortably, his cast probably taking up half the space, while I was over here practically folding myself in half just to avoid him.

This was ridiculous. I wasn't going to get any sleep like this. I'd be cranky and exhausted tomorrow, and the last thing I needed was to be short-tempered when Louie's restaurant was hanging by a thread.

I bit my lip, trying to resist the urge to just get up and crawl into the bed next to him. But the ache in my neck was becoming unbearable. I could feel the strain creeping up into my head, threatening a migraine, and the pillow… was it made of bricks?

I shifted again, and the loveseat let out another squeak.

There was a long pause, and I could hear him shifting in the bed, the rustle of sheets barely audible over the sound of my own breathing. I tossed and turned until, finally, I rolled onto the hard floor with an unceremonious thud.

I'd like to say Jordan snickered at my predicament. God, that would have made things so much easier. But he didn't. Instead, he had watched me with obvious growing concern that wrinkled his damned perfect face for a solid minute before finally whispering my name. "Annie."

Jordan's voice was soft but carried across the room like a whisper in the dark. I froze, my heart thudding as I turned toward him, eyes just able to make out his shape in the faint glow of the streetlight filtering through the curtains.

"You can't sleep like that," he said, his voice low, almost gentle.

"I'm fine," I lied, yanking the covers up over my shoulders, only to expose my toes.

Damn it.

"Annie," he said again, a touch more insistent this time. "Just get in the bed. We're both adults. It's not like we haven't done this before."

My cheeks burned at the memory of when we *had* shared a bed — back when things were simpler, back when we were... us. And now here we were, years later, pretending none of that mattered.

"That's what I'm afraid of," I muttered under my breath, half-hoping he didn't hear me.

But the bed let out a creak as he shifted again, and I knew he had.

I bit my lip, feeling my pulse quicken as I stared up at the ceiling. After fifteen minutes of trying to sleep on the loveseat, I finally caved.

I had to.

I was not a Murphy bed. The human body wasn't meant to fold like that, and I was feeling like I might snap in half. My body screamed for relief, and as much as I hated to admit it, he was right. We were adults. We could handle this.

Slowly, reluctantly, I pulled myself up, every muscle in my back protesting as I did. The room felt cooler outside of my makeshift blanket cocoon, and as I padded across the floor toward the bed, I could feel the chill of the hardwood under my bare feet.

Jordan shifted to make space for me, pulling the covers back slightly, and my stomach twisted as I hovered at the edge of the bed. The scent of him — faintly warm and familiar, like cedar and soap—reached me, stirring memories I'd been trying hard to bury.

I swallowed hard and slipped beneath the covers, my body stiff and awkward as I positioned myself as far to the edge as possible. The sheets were cool against my skin, and I could feel the warmth of his body from the other side of the bed, like a subtle heat radiating through the mattress. The air was thick with the weight of all the things unsaid between us, making every movement feel loaded with meaning.

I lay there, still and tense, staring up at the ceiling as my heart hammered in my chest. I could hear the soft rhythm of Jordan's breathing, feel the gentle rise and fall of the mattress as he settled back into place. The bed creaked faintly, and the air felt too close, too intimate.

It was different now. The last time we shared a bed, we'd been tangled in each other, lost in the heat of something new and exciting. But now? Now there was too much history. Too many memories.

I closed my eyes, trying to steady my breathing, but I could still sense him beside me— the warmth of him, the steady sound of his breaths, the familiar scent of him that made my chest tighten with longing I didn't want to acknowledge.

"Comfortable?" Jordan's voice was soft,

almost teasing, breaking the silence.

I hesitated, feeling the tension curl tighter inside me. "Yeah," I whispered back, though I wasn't sure if that was true. Physically, I was more comfortable than I'd been on the loveseat, but emotionally?

I felt like I was teetering on the edge of something dangerous.

"Good," he whispered, his voice low and warm. "Get some sleep, McGowan."

He called me by my last name, the way he always used to. It should have felt casual, playful, but the way his voice wrapped around it… it didn't. It felt intimate.

Too intimate.

I bit my lip and rolled over, turning my back to him and curling up on my side. I could still feel the faint warmth of his body behind me, could still hear the soft sound of his breathing, and my skin prickled with awareness.

As I lay there, my mind drifted back to everything I was trying to keep at bay. The competition. The lies. The feelings I wasn't supposed to have for him anymore. The guilt gnawed at me, sharper than the ache in my back had been, twisting deep inside my chest.

I wasn't sure how long I lay there, my mind spinning, but eventually, the warmth of the bed and the rhythmic sound of Jordan's breathing lulled me into a fitful sleep.

*****

When I woke up the next morning, the smell of burned toast hit me like a punch in the face.

Didn't you smell burned toast when you had a brain tumor?

For a second, I had forgotten my ex-boyfriend was staying in my apartment. But then everything came rushing back, and now it smelled like he had somehow set the kitchen on fire.

I stumbled out of bed, running into the kitchen, only to find Jordan standing in front of the toaster with a confused look on his face.

"I didn't touch anything," he said quickly, holding up his hands in surrender. "The toaster just... did that."

I frowned, stepping closer and eyeing the blackened slices of toast. I looked at the toaster's temperature dial and groaned.

"Of course," I muttered, rubbing my eyes. "The level one on this thing is more like a level five."

Jordan raised an eyebrow. "That's... concerning."

I shrugged. "It's all the thrift store had. This toaster has a mind of its own. Sometimes it gives you the perfect toast. Most of the time, it gives you charcoal."

Jordan shook his head, grinning. "I guess I won't be cooking breakfast then."

I sighed and grabbed the toast, tossing it into the trash. "It's not your fault. My appliances are just… special."

Jordan laughed, leaning against the counter as he watched me grab more bread from the pantry. "I'm getting that impression."

I shoved two more slices into the toaster, turning the dial down to where level one should have been. "Let's just hope it cooperates this time."

We stood in a comfortable silence as the toaster worked its magic—hopefully without turning the bread into ash.

Jordan cleared his throat after a moment. "So… how'd you sleep?"

I shot him a look. "Are you seriously asking that after watching me try to contort myself into a human pretzel on the loveseat?"

He laughed. "Okay, okay. But once you got into the bed?"

I paused, unsure how to answer. The truth was, it had been awkward—but not as awkward as I'd expected. I had slept better than I thought I would, even with Jordan next to me. But admitting that felt… *deliciously dangerous.*

"It was fine," I said nonchalantly, hoping he wouldn't push the subject.

Thankfully, he didn't.

The toaster dinged, and I cautiously peeked inside, relieved to find two perfectly golden slices of toast.

"Success!" I said triumphantly, holding up the plate.

Jordan gave me a mock round of applause. "See? I always said you're a culinary genius."

"Yeah, yeah," I muttered, but I couldn't help but smile. "Let's see if I can get through the rest of breakfast without burning the apartment down."

"While you do that, I need to see a man about a lizard." He hobbled toward the restroom as my face scrunched in distaste.

I looked down at the generic pieces of toast staring at me from the plate. Their simplicity offended my culinary sensibilities.

"I can do so much better than this," I muttered. I started digging through my refrigerator and cabinets.

If we were going to survive the morning, breakfast had to be done right, especially since the faulty appliances were proving to be typically unpredictable. But as I stood in the kitchen, staring at the ingredients spread out before me, I realized I wasn't just making breakfast.

I was making French toast.

Not just any French toast, but the kind Jordan had always loved—the kind I used to make on lazy weekends back when things were simple between us. My fingers brushed over the strawberries, the bottle of amaretto, and the heavy cream. I wasn't consciously trying to impress him, but as I mixed the ingredients, I couldn't deny the care I was putting into each step.

The smell of warm cinnamon and vanilla filled the small kitchen as I dipped thick slices of bread into the rich custard, coating them evenly.

Sizzle.

The moment the bread hit the hot skillet, it crackled, releasing a sweet, toasty scent that made my stomach rumble. I added a dash of amaretto to the cream I was whipping, the faint, nutty aroma swirling through the air.

As I whipped the cream into soft peaks, I couldn't help but think about the mornings we'd spent together back then—me cooking, him stealing bites when he thought I wasn't looking. The ease we'd had felt like another lifetime, but somehow, standing here, it didn't feel so far away. And that scared me.

What am I doing?

I was making this breakfast as if it was for us. As if nothing had changed. As if I hadn't lied to him about the competition, as if I wasn't hiding him from Trent.

Why was it so easy to fall back into this rhythm with him?

It wasn't just breakfast, or the shared laughter — it was the way he looked at me, like no time had passed, like we hadn't left so much unsaid.

As I plated the French toast, the sense of unease lingered, like a thread I couldn't quite unravel. I wiped my hands on a dishtowel and glanced toward the bathroom, wondering what was taking Jordan so long.

My hands worked on autopilot, sprinkling powdered sugar over the top and arranging the fresh strawberries around the edges. The whipped cream — light, airy, and laced with amaretto — was spooned delicately over the toast, pooling perfectly like something you'd see in a magazine.

Why was I doing this? Why was I putting so much effort into something so trivial?

Maybe it was my way of apologizing for the guilt gnawing at me, for the secret I was keeping. Or maybe it was because, despite everything, part of me wanted to make him smile the way he used to when I cooked for him.

I set two plates on the tiny kitchen table and glanced toward the bathroom door.

I should check on him.

I made my way toward the bathroom,

knocking softly on the door. "Jordan? Breakfast is ready."

No response.

I frowned, hesitating for a moment before reaching for the door handle. It was slightly ajar, so I pushed it open gently.

"Jordan?"

And then I froze.

Standing before me was Jordan, but not in the way I expected. He was fresh out of the shower, water still beading down his chest, and — oh God — he was completely naked except for the garbage bag he'd secured over his cast to keep it dry.

For a split second, I couldn't move. My brain went into full shutdown mode, caught somewhere between mortification and utter shock.

"Annie!" Jordan yelped, scrambling for the towel, but the slick floor betrayed him. Before I could react, his cast leg caught on the rug, and he toppled forward — straight into me. My back hit the tub, water splashing everywhere as we collapsed into a heap of limbs and crinkling garbage bag. The garbage bag whined like a deflating balloon as Jordan flailed, and a cold splash of water hit my face, making me sputter as I tried to wriggle out from beneath him.

"Jordan!" I gasped, trying to push him off me but laughing despite myself. "What the —"

"I'm so sorry!" he groaned, clearly just as mortified as I was. He tried to get up, but with the wet floor, his cast, and our general lack of coordination, he only made things worse. We both ended up in a tangled heap, still stuck in the tub, and the ridiculousness of the situation hit me.

I couldn't stop laughing. The absurdity of it all—naked Jordan, the garbage bag, the fall—was too much. The laughter bubbled up uncontrollably, and soon Jordan was laughing too, though his face was bright red.

"I swear I was just trying to clean up!" he managed between fits of laughter, still half-tangled in the curtain. "Not put on a peep show."

"I'm not sure what's more hysterical—the fall or this garbage bag look you're rocking," I teased, wiping tears of laughter from my eyes.

He grinned sheepishly as we finally pulled him from the tub, though he was still wobbling slightly. "You're the one who walked in without knocking."

"I *did* knock!" I protested, but the laugh that escaped my lips betrayed any seriousness I'd been trying to convey.

Jordan looked down at himself, then back at me, his grin widening. "Well, this wasn't exactly how I envisioned the morning going."

I groaned, finally sitting up and pushing myself out of the tub, my clothes soaked. "You and me both."

We stood there for a moment, still chuckling, both of us dripping wet and trying to catch our breath. The bathroom was a disaster, and we were an even bigger one.

"Let's just pretend this never happened," I said, shaking my head. But judging by Jordan's sheepish grin, we both knew it was unforgettable.

And that was the naked truth.

Chapter Twelve

Jordan

Annie's apartment was small. Not just in size — that much was obvious. It was small in a way that felt temporary — like it wasn't a destination but a stop along the way. The mismatched furniture, the thrift store appliances, the muted tones that didn't scream Annie... it all felt like she was holding her breath, waiting for something to begin.

Or maybe, waiting for something to end.

She'd left for work, making me promise not to touch the toaster. Now, I hobbled around, restless, trying to make sense of what her life had become — and what that meant for us.

If there even was an "us" anymore.

My crutches squeaked slightly against the floor as I glanced at the details scattered around the room. A chipped ceramic mug that read: *Coffee is my love language*. A half-finished paint-by-numbers canvas propped against the wall, its vibrant colors clashing with the drab beige surroundings. A magnet on the fridge that read *Don't quit your daydream.* Small things that felt like her, trying to break through.

I wasn't snooping. Not really. Just... looking. My eyes caught on a trinket box tucked behind a couple of books on the shelf. Carefully, I lifted the lid. Inside were small keepsakes—a delicate bracelet, postcards, a couple of concert tickets. And one thing that hit me like a sucker punch: a worn-out ticket stub from the Kansas State Fair. *The* Kansas State Fair.

My throat tightened.

I remembered that day. We'd spent it laughing, stuffing our faces with fried everything, and riding the Ferris wheel until we were dizzy. I'd taken the day off from the farm—a rare thing. Annie had convinced me to skip my chores and come along, and for once, I was glad she did. That was one of the last days before everything got... complicated.

She kept this?

I put the ticket back carefully, closing the box like it held something fragile. My gaze shifted to the pictures on the shelf. Most of them were new, taken after she moved to New York—photos with coworkers, charity events, brunches with smiling friends. And there was him. Trent.

I picked up a framed photo of the two of

them — Trent in his pristine suit, standing beside Annie at some gala. She was smiling, but not in the way I remembered. This smile was polished. Perfect. Less... her.

"This guy?" I muttered under my breath, setting the frame back. Frustration bubbled in my chest. Trent wasn't the guy for her. I didn't even know the guy, and I was sure of it. My hand reached for another picture, this one half-hidden behind a stack of cookbooks.

It was us. Annie and me, back in Kansas. Covered in flour in Granny McGowan's kitchen, laughing like idiots after trying — and failing — to bake her famous scones. Annie had flung a handful of flour at me after I'd teased her about over mixing the dough. Her grin had been wild and unfiltered, her cheeks pink from laughing too hard.

That was before everything changed. Before I let her go.

I hadn't walked away. Not exactly. I'd let her leave, thinking it was for the best. Thinking my career — or what I wanted my career to become — mattered more than she ever could. And now, standing here, I knew how wrong I'd been. I'd made it easy for her to think I didn't care when, in truth, I cared too much.

The knock at the door startled me, jolting me out of the past. I hobbled over, peering through the peephole, part of me hoping maybe it was Trent.

It wasn't.

I opened the door to an older woman bundled in a thick knit navy cardigan and Cobbie Cuddlers. Bright eyes smiles behind thick glasses as she stood there, holding a Tupperware of something that looked like soup with golf balls floating in it.

"Oh, look at you," she said, shaking her head. "Poor boy, standing there with that leg. I brought you some matza ball soup. Good for the body, and good for the soul." She handed me the container like it was a sacred offering.

I chuckled and stumbled slightly as she pushed me aside. "Thank you?"

"It's nothing," she explained, immediately grabbing two bowls and two spoons from the dish drainer beside the sink. "I'm Mrs. Katz. 2B."

"I'm Jordan. Not 2B," I replied, still a little shocked at this woman's familiarity. She reminded me of someone.

Granny McGowan.

That was it. I guess Annie had drawn people close that reminded her of home.

"Ah," Mrs. Katz held up a finger. "Shakespeare. Smart boy. I'm sure your *bubbe* would be proud."

I wasn't exactly trying to quote the bard,

but I didn't bother correcting her. "I'm Jordan, by the way. Annie's... well, I'm a friend."

"A friend, huh?" She plopped into a kitchen chair like she owned the place, clunking the bowls on the table. "Well, I'm her friend too. But I'm also your friend now. Here. Sit. Eat. We'll talk."

Before I could argue, she was already spooning soup into the bowls, motioning for me to sit beside her. I obeyed, balancing awkwardly on the chair as she handed me a spoon.

"Matza ball soup. You eat," she declared, like it was law.

I took a bite—warm, savory, comforting in a way I didn't expect. "This is incredible."

She waved a hand. "Of course it's incredible. I've been making it for seventy years. Now, tell me, Jordan. What are you doing here, in this tiny apartment? A boy from Kansas, a chef— eh, I've heard of you."

I paused mid-bite. "You've heard of me?"

"Annie talks about you," she stated, folding her hands in her lap. "Not often, but enough. She's proud of what you've done, you know."

The spoon hovered in my hand as her words sank in.

Annie talked about me?

It wasn't much, but it meant something— something I hadn't let myself hope for. Maybe I wasn't as forgotten as I'd feared.

I cleared my throat, trying to keep my voice steady. "I'm here for a competition. Whisk It All, actually. It's a big deal."

Her eyebrows lifted. "A competition? And this will help Annie how?"

"Well," I began, leaning back, "the prize money—it's enough to help Annie open her own restaurant. It's her dream—always has been."

Her sharp eyes softened. "Ah. So, it's not just about you."

I shook my head, feeling the weight of it all pressing down on me. "No. I made a mistake a long time ago. I'm trying to make things right."

She leaned closer, her expression serious. "What went wrong?"

"I let her go," I admitted, the words heavy. "I thought she'd be better off without me. Thought my life in Kansas would hold her back. I thought it would be easier if she thought I didn't care."

Mrs. Katz let out a knowing sigh. "Men. Always think they're doing what's best by saying nothing. And when they finally realize they've made a mess, the woman's halfway gone."

I smiled wryly at her bluntness. "You're not wrong."

"And now she's engaged to Trent." Her lips curled in a wry smile. "I've met him. Handsome boy, but not for Annie. Too… perfect."

"You think so?" I asked, surprised.

She shrugged. "Annie is fire. Trent? He wants to put out the flame. You? You want to feed it."

The knot in my chest loosened. "I came here to win. For her. I want to prove I'm not the guy she left behind."

She patted my hand. "Good. Then fight for her."

Her chair scraped the linoleum as she backed away from the table and stood. "I must go." She handed me a slip of paper. "Here's my number, if you need anything."

"Wait. You're leaving?" I gestured to her full bowl. "But you've hardly touched your soup."

She smiled. "It's for you. Eat up. You're going to need your strength if you're going to fight for her."

Fight for her?

Mrs. Katz shuffled toward the door. Her gnarled hand reached out to turn the knob, and she turned. "Eat. Feed the flame."

She opened the door and walked out into the hall, giving me a cheery wave before closing it and leaving me with about a gallon of soup.

Her words stayed with me long after she'd left. I turned to my duffel bag, ready to dive into my notes and remind myself why I was here. But as I unzipped the bag, my chest tightened.

Where the hell…?

I searched through the pockets, my hands growing frantic. Clothes, toiletries—everything was there. But the competition materials?

Gone.

Chapter Thirteen

Annie

The morning air was cool and crisp as I made my way to Vitello's, my nose catching the warm, buttery scent wafting from the corner bakery. I could hear the rumble of the trash truck down the block, the faint hum of sleepy conversations between neighbors opening up shop. Normally, this stretch of the street felt like home, each step carrying me a little closer to where I belonged. Today, though, it felt more like I was trudging through quicksand, each step sinking me deeper into the mess my life had somehow become.

Jordan.

A deep breath barely helped quell the flutter of nerves his name sent straight to my stomach. He was camped out on my couch, propped up with his broken leg and a whole heap of unresolved feelings we'd both left in Kansas.

And then there was Trent—my fiancé. Oh, God, my fiancé—blissfully unaware that his future wife's ex was back in her life in the most inconvenient, immobile way possible.

As if all of that wasn't enough, there was Louie, Vitello's owner, and the closest thing I had to family in this city. He was one bank notice away from losing the restaurant, his whole life's work, and I could practically feel the weight of it crushing be into the pavement.

The universe had clearly handed me a perfect storm. All I needed was some kind of sign, a user's manual on managing a fiancé, an ex-boyfriend, and a failing restaurant all at once. But maybe the real plan was just to keep going until everything exploded.

Because what did it matter then?

When I pushed open the heavy glass door to Vitello's, an uneasy quiet filled the air. Usually, Louie would be at the front, giving me a big wave or calling out a cheerful, "*Buongiorno*, Annie!" before diving back into whatever culinary chaos he'd left simmering on the stove. But today, the space was strangely quiet, and Louie wasn't behind the counter or in the kitchen.

I finally spotted him slouching over a table in the corner, his broad shoulders sagging, a piece of paper clutched tightly in his hand. My heart sank. Louie had always been a steady force—never one to slump or brood. Even on his hardest days, he'd shrug things off with a "We'll figure it out," or a joke to lighten the mood. But right now, he looked like a man carrying the weight of the world, and something told me he wasn't ready to shrug anything off this morning.

"Louie?" I approached him slowly, and his head jerked, as if he hadn't even heard me come in. He gave me a tired smile, but his eyes were shadowed, worry lines creasing his usually warm face.

"Ah, *buongiorno*, *ragazza*," he said, trying for his usual cheer, but it didn't reach his eyes. He held up the paper, his fingers crinkling the edges. "Look at this. We get a little, uh, visitor—a 'friendly' note from the bank." He gave a bitter chuckle.

I didn't need to ask. The words "balloon payment" flashed across my mind, followed by the sharp realization that this was it—the final countdown for Vitello's. I pulled out a chair and sat across from him, reaching out to place my hand over his, hoping I could somehow keep this place, this life, from slipping away.

Louie sighed, sliding the crumpled paper across the table toward me. "There it is," he mumbled, his voice carrying the weight of someone who had seen more than his fair share of hard times. "They want their money by the end of the week, or…" He trailed off, unable to finish the sentence.

I looked down at the letter, each word feeling like a punch to the gut. *Final notice... outstanding balance... must be paid in full.* The demands were brutal, heartless. My gaze drifted back up to Louie, who looked older than I'd ever seen him. The creases around his eyes seemed deeper, his shoulders more slumped, as if every ounce of energy had been sapped from him by this one piece of paper.

"They can't do this," I said, shaking my head. "Vitello's is... it's part of the neighborhood. This place has been here forever. People love it here."

He gave a small, sad smile. "Ah, Annie, the bank don't care about love. All they care about is money." He shrugged, trying to put on a brave face, but his expression betrayed him. "I've been through hard times before, *ragazza*, but this..." His voice broke, just a little, and he took a deep breath. "This might be the end."

My heart sank as I absorbed the reality of his words. The thought of Vitello's—Louie's life's work, the beating heart of our little community— just... gone. It felt like losing a piece of myself.

"Louie..." I started, but I didn't know what to say. I wanted to reassure him, to tell him we'd find a way, but the words felt hollow.

Desperate to see even a hint of hope in his eyes, I leaned forward, clasping my hands. "Louie, what if we hold a fundraiser? A big community dinner, something everyone can be a part of. People love Vitello's! They'll show up and pitch in to keep this place alive."

I could already picture it—the tables filled with loyal customers, laughter and conversation bouncing off the walls, plates piled high with Louie's signature dishes, and a donation jar overflowing with contributions from people who had been coming here for years. We could even have a raffle, maybe a tasting event—anything to keep the doors open.

Louie gave a small, sad chuckle, looking down at his hands. "Ah, *ragazza*, I appreciate it," he murmured. "But people got their own troubles. They come here to forget them, not to add more." He glanced around the quiet restaurant, and his expression softened, as if he were already saying goodbye. "It's too late, Annie. Maybe it's time to let go."

Louie looked down, tracing the edge of the table with his finger, lost in thought. When he finally spoke, his voice was low, almost reverent. "Valentine's Day," he said, with a sad smile. "It's fitting, don't you think? A day about love… it'll be the last for Vitello's. One last night with our regulars, with family. Then we'll close for good."

The finality of it grabbed me like someone had ripped my heart from my chest. Valentine's

Day was just around the corner, and Louie—who had put every ounce of himself into this place—was ready to let it go. I searched his face for some glimmer of doubt, some part of him still willing to fight, but his expression was calm, resigned. He'd made peace with it.

"Louie, it doesn't have to end like this," I whispered, hoping my voice could break through. But he patted my hand gently, as if comforting me instead of himself.

"Sometimes, *ragazza*," he said softly, "we have to know when to say goodbye."

As he shuffled back toward the kitchen, shoulders slumped, resignation hanging on him like a heavy coat, something sparked inside a mix of anger and determination. No way was I going to let Vitello's go down without a fight. Not now. Not after all Louie had put into it.

I took a deep breath, clenching my fists as if I could hold on to this sudden surge of resolve. *I'm not letting you give up, Louie.* If winning that Whisk It All prize was our only shot, then I was going all in.

This was our lifeline, our last chance, and I'd do whatever it took to save this place. When all was said and done Louie would look back at that bank notice and laugh. He'd have his restaurant, and I'd make damn sure of it.

I took a deep breath, letting it fill me up and

squash all the tangled emotions clawing at me. I couldn't let myself fall apart—not here and not now. Louie needed me to keep it together, even if he didn't realize it yet.

Forcing a smile, I adjusted my apron and walked into the kitchen, determined to shake off the weight of that bank notice. The regulars would be coming in soon, expecting comfort on a plate, and no matter what storm was brewing behind the scenes, Vitello's still had to feel like the place they all loved.

Curtis was already at the stove, stirring the tomato basil soup with his usual laser focus, the rich aroma filling the room. I gave him a nod, grabbed my station, and fell into the familiar rhythm of prep work. With each chop, stir, and taste, I felt myself sink into the steady, calming routine. Whatever happened tomorrow, today I'd give Vitello's everything I had.

As I chopped fresh basil, the rhythmic thunk of the knife against the cutting board should've been soothing. But with each slice, my mind drifted further from Vitello's. Instead, it was back in my apartment, sneaking a look at the competition paperwork I'd borrowed from Jordan's duffel.

Borrowed. Right.

I let out a sigh. The guilt creeped in like a shadow. Sneaking my way in under Jordan's name. Taking his shot. Twisting his dream into my Hail Mary pass to save Vitello's. I straightened with sudden, enlightening validation.

He did it to me.

He had yanked my blue ribbon out from under me. And with my recipe.

What did I have to feel guilty about?

Besides, this was for all the right reasons. Vitello's wasn't just a restaurant. It was a lifeline, a place that gave people joy, comfort, and community. If winning this competition could keep that alive, then I'd face Jordan's anger later. Maybe someday he'd even forgive me.

That last thought caught me off guard.

Why in the hell did I care?

I ran my hands over the chopped basil, breathing in the fresh, peppery scent, hoping it would ground me. This isn't about betraying Jordan, I told myself, though the words felt thin.

It's about fighting for something worth saving.

The guilt started creeping back in.

Maybe he wouldn't even realize I took it.

Just as I was starting to convince myself this plan was manageable — just as I was really leaning into my 'it's for the greater good' mentality — my phone buzzed in my apron pocket. I glanced at the screen, expecting maybe a text from Trent about the wedding or, at worst, a reminder from the bank about Vitello's looming deadline. But no. It was from Jordan.

Damn. He still had my number

JORDAN: Hey. Did you see some papers I left in my duffel? I had a few things I need to double-check.

My heart practically jumped into my throat, pounding against my ribcage with the force of a runaway train. I gripped my phone tighter, my mind racing through a dozen ways to respond without sounding suspicious.

My fingers hovered over the screen, too stiff to type. My rationalizing from moments ago suddenly felt flimsy, the guilt bubbling up so fast I could barely swallow it down. I was in deeper than I'd thought, and now Jordan was digging.

I stared at the screen, my mind racing, trying to find the perfect combination of words that would satisfy Jordan without raising his suspicions. Every phrase I considered sounded guilty or evasive. My nerves ratcheted up with each second that ticked by. Finally, I typed.

ME: If it was in your bag, I'm sure it's around somewhere. Don't worry about it.

I hit send before I could second-guess myself. I set my phone face down on the counter, taking a deep breath to steady myself. It wasn't exactly a lie… I hadn't technically lost his paperwork, just… repurposed it.

I told myself he'd probably forget about it or find something else to focus on. Jordan was the kind of guy who let little things slide, so maybe he'd let this go. But the churn in my stomach didn't settle, and I braced for the next text, wondering if he'd push further.

The competition was days away. I only had to keep him in the dark a little longer — just long enough to win.

I'd barely set my phone down when it buzzed again. My stomach flipped. Jordan would not let this go.

But it wasn't Jordan. Trent's name flashed across the screen. My eyes flew wide.

He knew about Jordan!

I sighed, bracing myself to answer a barrage of questions about the strange man in my apartment.

TRENT: Hey, babe! Quick question. Should we put the Graysons at table seven?

I rolled my eyes, trying not to laugh.

Who in the hell were the Graysons?

On a 500-person guest list that Trent and his mother had compiled, including every distant cousin and business contact they could think of, I had exactly two people coming to this wedding: Louie and Curtis. The whole seating arrangement was a circus of tables I barely recognized.

I tapped out a response.

ME: I don't care.

But my finger hovered over the send button. After a second, I deleted it and sent something more neutral.

ME: I trust whatever you think is best.

I was really feeling like the wedding was turning into a show I'd been cast in, and apparently, I'd agreed to seating arrangements I hadn't even known existed.

A few seconds later, my phone buzzed again. Expecting another wedding detail, I glanced down, only to see that Trent had taken the conversation in a different direction.

TRENT: What's cooking today?

ME: Puttanesca.

TRENT: Mmmm. Wait till you see what I'm going to be *puttanesca-in* you on the honeymoon.

I raised my eyebrow, caught off guard. Trent wasn't usually one for flirty texts.

TRENT: I've been cooking up a few ideas for us… let's just say I plan to keep things *simmering*.

I couldn't help but grin.

ME: Oh really? Now you've got me curious. 😳

TRENT: Better be ready — It's gonna get a little spicy. 😏

I bit back a laugh. This was a side of Trent I didn't see often, and I had to admit, it was a nice break from all his usual Type A behavior.

My phone buzzed again just as I was setting it down, Jordan's name flashing on the screen. I quickly opened it, his text short and to the point.

JORDAN: So, you're sure you haven't seen the paperwork anywhere?

I chewed on my lip, my mind scrambling for an answer that wouldn't give anything away. The puttanesca bubbled on the stove, the aroma of garlic and tomatoes wafting through the kitchen. My phone buzzed again, pulling me back into the whirlwind of texts.

TRENT: By the way, don't get too full — I've got dessert planned for later. 😜

I bit my lip, shaking my head with a grin. My thumbs hovered over the keyboard as Curtis's voice broke through the din.

"Annie, the soup's ready for plating! You good over there?"

"Yeah," I called back, turning my attention to the simmering pot. I stirred absently. My thoughts split between the sauce in front of me and the texts lighting up my screen.

My phone buzzed again, Jordan's name flashing this time. I froze, my heart skipping. The heat from the stove suddenly felt oppressive as I juggled the bubbling pot, Curtis's questions, and the growing weight of Jordan's inquiries.

JORDAN: Can't find it anywhere.

Every buzz felt like a new level of juggling, trying to keep one conversation vague and the other flirty. And somehow, I had to keep an eye on the kitchen, where the puttanesca was close to boiling over.

"Annie! Heads up, the lunch rush is starting!" Curtis's shout pulled me back to reality, but my mind was scattered, split between simmering pots and texts that threatened to spill over.

As I flipped between Trent's flirtatious messages and Jordan's increasingly probing questions about his missing paperwork, I felt like I was juggling a thousand things at once. My fingers flew over the screen, trying to keep up with both conversations while stirring a pot with my free hand.

TRENT: And don't forget, I've got a few *saucy* surprises for you.

JORDAN: I could use an extra set of hands when you get home.

I smirked, feeling cheeky, and fired back.

ME: I'll be ready with a side of extra spice, just the way you like it. 🤏

The instant I hit send, my stomach dropped as I watched the message go……straight to Jordan.

I froze, horrified.

Oh no, no, no......

My mind raced as I pictured Jordan's reaction, probably staring at his phone with one eyebrow raised, reading into every single word.

An eggplant emoji?

This was a man who knew how to read between the lines — and I'd just sent him the wrong script.

I stared at the screen in panic, dreading the moment those three little dots appeared, signaling his response.

I held the red pepper flake shaker over the pot, hovering as I waited for his reply...and the dots disappeared. Relief flooded over me until the phone buzzed again.

JORDAN: 😳......🍑

The lid of the pepper shaker came loose, dumping the entire contents of the container into my bubbling puttanesca. I groaned.

Spicy, indeed.

Chapter Fourteen

Trent

"Son, you need to start thinking more like a business owner and less like a groom."

My father's words hung in the air, sharp and condescending as always. I sat across from him in his office in Midtown, the sprawling cityscape behind him nothing but a backdrop for the real power in the room—him. Douglas Parker. The man who built the Parker empire and expected nothing less than perfection from anyone carrying his name. He'd wasted no time getting here when his flight had arrived from Long Island.

"This wedding of yours," he continued, flipping through the folder of wedding plans I'd laid before him. "It's fine. Necessary, even. But don't lose sight of what really matters."

"Annie is a great fit," I replied, straightening in my chair. "For both the new restaurant and the company."

He leaned back, steepling his fingers as he regarded me with the cold, appraising stare I knew too well. "She had better be."

Of course, he didn't mean a fit for me, not in the way that mattered. To him, Annie wasn't my fiancée, my partner, the woman I'd chosen. She was a calculated move. A strategic hire. Someone with enough talent and charisma to be the face of the Parker brand's latest venture.

"And you're certain she'll be on board once Vitello's is gone?" His voice was devoid of concern, as though the restaurant wasn't a piece of Annie's heart and history. It was just another property to be acquired, flattened, and rebuilt into something more profitable.

"She'll understand," I said evenly. "Once Vitello's is behind her, she'll see that the new restaurant is her best option."

Father raised an eyebrow, his lips curling faintly. "You make it sound like you're doing her a favor."

I fought to keep my tone neutral. "I am. We are. This is an opportunity she'd never get on her own."

That sounded convincing, didn't it?

I wasn't manipulating Annie. I was giving her something better. Something she deserved.

He didn't reply immediately, and the silence stretched, pressing down on me like the weight of the city itself. Finally, he leaned forward, his voice low and sharp. "She's only an asset if she plays her part. Keep her focused, Trent. Don't let sentimentality derail the plan."

The word "sentimentality" landed like a slap. My father saw nothing beyond profit margins and leverage. To him, Annie's passion— her connection to Vitello's—meant nothing.

"She won't be a problem," I restated firmly.

I told myself this was just business. Nothing personal. But when I saw Annie pulling a double shift at Vitello's, exhaustion lining her face, something in my gut always twisted. The Parker way meant taking control, ensuring success at all costs. But for the first time, I wondered if my father's version of success was a gilded cage—and if I'd been locked inside it for years without realizing it.

My father's eyes narrowed, and I braced myself for the inevitable. "Good. We've worked too hard to get here. Don't let her—or anyone— jeopardize what we've built."

The conversation shifted to logistics, dates, and deadlines. But my mind wandered, replaying his words over and over.

Don't let her get in the way. Keep her in line.

*****

The late afternoon sun cast long shadows over the street as I pulled up outside Vitello's. For a moment, I stayed in the car, staring at the faded red awning. To my father, this was nothing but a crumbling building — an investment that had outlived its usefulness. But I knew better. It meant more than that to some people.

Annie had poured years into this place. She'd spent countless hours perfecting recipes, building relationships with customers, and crafting something that felt... personal. I knew it mattered to her, even if I didn't fully understand why.

I sighed, leaning against the hood of my car. The harder I tried to see Vitello's through her eyes, the more my father's words drowned everything out.

A failing business is a liability.

The smell of garlic and baking bread drifted through the air, mixing with the faint laughter of a couple leaving the restaurant.

"Every time we come here, Louie remembers our order," the woman said, her voice warm.

"Yeah," her companion replied. "Feels like home."

Their words made me squirm. This wasn't just food to Annie. It wasn't even just a career. It was a connection — to people, to history, to something that felt alive in a way my father's spreadsheets never could.

For her, Vitello's wasn't failing. It was thriving, but in a manner the balance sheets couldn't show. I wanted to see it that way, too. I just didn't know how.

I wanted to see it through her eyes. To meet her there. But the harder I tried, the louder my father's voice got. I sighed, shifting my weight.

Why couldn't she see the opportunity in letting go?

I didn't get it. Not completely. But I wanted to. I wanted to be the kind of man who could meet her where she was. A man who could see what she saw.

The problem was, I didn't know how.

*****

By the time I got home, the city's noise had dulled into a low drone. My apartment felt curated. Impersonal. I tossed my keys onto the counter. The sound echoed too loudly in the quiet space.

The city lights flickered against the glass, a cold, distant glow. Annie's warmth was so different. The way her eyes lit up whenever she talked about Vitello's. She didn't just care about food—she cared about the people who made it and shared it.

I pulled out my phone, hesitating. I wanted

to talk to her about it. To understand what this place meant to her. Maybe then I'd have some ammunition to take to my father. But how could I ask without sounding wrong?

Instead, I typed something simpler.

ME: What's cooking today?

Her reply came almost instantly.

ANNIE: Puttanesca.

I smiled despite myself, picturing her in Vitello's kitchen, her hair pulled back, her hands moving effortlessly through ingredients.

For a moment, I almost typed something more.

ME: I'm sorry. I understand now.

But my thumb hesitated over the keys. Words like that didn't come easily — not to a Parker.

Instead, I let myself believe that this could all work out. That I could be the man she needed, not the man my father expected me to be.

Chapter Fifteen

Jordan

Annie's unexpected text lit up my screen, and I read it twice, just to be sure I hadn't misinterpreted things. A little playful, a little bold, and maybe — just maybe — something more. The eggplant emoji caught my attention, making me raise an eyebrow. This was Annie, after all. Not exactly one to throw out emojis like that unless there was something she wanted me to know. I couldn't help but smirk, a grin spreading across my face.

If she was still interested, maybe there was hope for us after all. I leaned back, fingers tapping out a reply with confidence I hadn't felt in a long time. After hitting "SEND" I waited, anticipation running through me like electricity, imagining her reaction. She'd blush, she'd laugh — but definitely wouldn't be able to ignore that message.

Her response took a while, but that was okay. I was in no hurry. I was busy imagining how things would be different this time. Back in Kansas, I'd let her walk away, thinking the worst of me. Let her think my priorities were all backward because I'd been too damn proud to tell her my plans weren't just for me.

They had been for us.

This time, though, I was ready to do it right. Show her I'd come back to make things right and see us both end up where we were supposed to be. With her at my side.

But first, there was one minor problem.

I had to find my competition credentials.

I scanned around Annie's small apartment, trying to remember where I'd last seen the paperwork. I could've sworn I'd left it in my duffel bag, but after the run-in with her neighbor, Mrs. Katz, and moving things around while hobbling on this damn broken leg, it could be anywhere. For a brief second, a wild thought crossed my mind: what if Annie had found it and taken it? I mean, she had been acting a little... weird.

An eggplant, huh?

I smirked again, remembering the emoji and her playful tone. No, there was no way she'd swipe my invitation and then send suggestive messages. Annie might be a mystery sometimes, but she wasn't that complicated.

I made a mental note to call the competition

coordinator in the morning to confirm my entry, just in case. Right now, though, there was something more important at hand.

Dinner.

I glanced at the clock, figuring Annie would be home soon. She was probably exhausted, with everything going on at the restaurant and her endless wedding planning with Trent. The thought made me grimace. But tonight, I wanted to do something nice for her, to remind her I could still make her smile — and that she'd chosen me once for a reason.

I headed to the fridge with as much of a stride as I could muster on one leg, feeling determined to pull off a proper meal for her. I opened the door, only to be greeted by... well, disappointment. A few wilting vegetables, half a carton of milk, and more takeout containers than I could count.

I chuckled, muttering to myself. "Classic Annie."

It was slim pickings, to say the least. But then a thought struck me. *Matzo ball soup.* The cure for what ails ya. The thought of making it for Annie felt oddly fitting.

And who better to help me than Mrs. Katz, the self-appointed soup queen of the apartment building?

Mrs. Katz hadn't been wrong. I had felt

better after the first bowl of the soup she had brought. Even better after the second. By the third, I was a new man... and the Tupperware was empty.

I dialed her number, and she answered on the second ring.

"Mrs. Katz, it's Jordan. I was wondering if you could help me with something... I'm trying to make matzo ball soup for Annie."

"Ah! Matzo ball soup! Good boy." I could hear her Pepsodent grin through the phone. "Every girl needs soup made for her once in a while. Sure, sure, I'll bring everything you need." Her enthusiasm made me smile, and within a few minutes, she knocked on the door, arms full of ingredients and a gleam of excitement in her eyes.

"Oh, we're going to make a good soup, my boy!" She bustled in, unpacking ingredients and immediately taking charge of the tiny kitchen.

Under Mrs. Katz's watchful eye, I followed her instructions, rolling up my sleeves and trying to remember everything she told me. She showed me how to mix the matzo meal, eggs, and just the right amount of *schmaltz*, emphasizing that "a good matzo ball is fluffy, not heavy." I tried to follow her lead, but as I shaped the balls, they looked less like spheres and more like lumpy potatoes.

"Not bad," she said, chuckling as she

inspected my handiwork. "A little practice and you'll make perfect matzo balls yet."

"Don't go planning the *bar mitzvah* yet, Mrs. Katz."

We laughed together as I tried my best. The air filled with the smell of onions and chicken broth. She shared stories of her late husband, who'd cooked the same soup for her when they were newlyweds. Her laughter was contagious, and before long, I relaxed, grateful for the unexpected company.

Mrs. Katz handed me the ladle. "Here, you stir. Slowly and don't rush—good soup needs time to work its magic."

"Yes, ma'am," I said, trying to look serious as I stirred, and she patted my shoulder.

As we worked, she cast me a knowing look. "So, tell me, Jordan... what's got you cooking up a storm for our Annie, hmm?"

I cleared my throat, not expecting the question. "Just trying to show her I still care," I admitted, surprised at how easily the words came.

"Good boy," she said again, patting my arm. "Now, remember, a girl's heart is a lot like a good soup. Can't rush it. Needs patience, time to simmer." She winked, leaving the advice to hang in the air.

Once the soup was simmering, Mrs. Katz stood back and gave me an approving nod.

"There, you've done it. Now just let it rest a bit. She's one lucky girl to come home to this."

"Thank you, Mrs. Katz. Really. Couldn't have done it without you."

She grinned and patted my arm. "I'll keep an ear out to see if you need help to finish the soup." And with that, she slipped out the door, leaving me in the quiet of Annie's apartment, watching the steam rise from the pot.

The soup smelled perfect. The rich, warm aroma filled the space. I glanced around, spotting a few candles in a cupboard. I figured a little ambiance wouldn't hurt. I set the table, arranged the bowls, and lit the candles, making the whole setup feel… cozy. Like the dinners we used to have, just the two of us, no other plans, no one else to think about.

I sat back, waiting, imagining her face when she walked in. There was so much to say. So much I wanted her to know. But for tonight, maybe a bowl of soup would be enough.

I had no idea what tomorrow would bring or how things would pan out with the competition. With Trent. With everything. But tonight, sitting here waiting for her, I felt more certain than I had in a long time.

Chapter Sixteen

Trent

The grocery list crinkled in my hand as I waited by the entrance of Rivera's Market, watching Annie dart from shelf to shelf like she was on a mission. I'd seen her shop dozens of times, and it was usually a quick affair—a bit of fresh produce, some eggs, bread, and a few essentials for Vitello's. But today was different. She was piling twice the usual amount into the cart and not just staples. She'd thrown in two gigantic bags of flour, extra vegetables, a pack of dry yeast, pickles…

… and chocolate ice cream?

"Annie," I said, raising an eyebrow as she placed yet another bag of rice in the cart, "I know you love to cook, but isn't this a little overboard?"

She blinked, momentarily surprised, before shrugging it off with a smile. "What can I say? A girl's got to eat, and Vitello's is busier than ever lately."

Vitello's busy? That didn't sound right.

I chuckled, trying to brush off the odd feeling gnawing at me. But something didn't quite add up. Annie wasn't the type to stock up like this unless she had a very specific plan. I glanced at the cart, considering her sudden enthusiasm. Not that I minded, but it felt... unusual.

And then it hit me, a thought that lodged itself in my mind and refused to leave. There was one thing that ramped up a woman's appetite.

Could she be pregnant?

The idea stuck, and as she tossed in another bag of vegetables, I couldn't help but blurt it out. "Annie... is there something you're not telling me?" I tried to keep my voice casual, even though my brain was already spiraling into possibilities I wasn't entirely sure I wanted.

She froze, looking at me with wide eyes.

I took her hands in mine and gazed at her lovingly. "You can tell me anything, you know."

Her eyes pulled away, darting around the store, before staring at the floor. "I...I wouldn't even know where to begin." She exhaled. "I knew this was going to be hard..."

"If you're worried about fitting into your wedding dress, a few more days won't matter, sweetheart. I mean, look," I gazed at her taut belly. "You're hardly even showing."

That earned me an abrupt scowl that slowly melted into humor.

"Wait… you think I'm pregnant?" Her laugh was awkward, but there was a flicker of shock there, too, as if the thought hadn't crossed her mind.

"Well… maybe? You're buying enough food to feed a small army," I joked, trying to lighten the mood, though a part of me was seriously wondering. I picked up the pickles and ice cream, holding them aloft. "And pickles and Chunky Monkey?"

She shook her head, her cheeks pink. "I promise, it's not that," she said, sounding amused but not entirely thrilled. "I'm just… you know, getting extra supplies. For the competition."

"The what?" Her tone had me more taken aback than the mention of a competition.

She didn't look at me, her focus on arranging the items in the cart, but her voice picked up a notch, the enthusiasm barely contained. "I entered the Whisk It All competition," she announced, her eyes sparkling. "It's this big cooking challenge with a cash prize. I figured, why not give it a shot?"

I nodded slowly, processing this. She looked genuinely excited, and that was great. But the timing couldn't be worse.

"The Whisk It All competition. Right." I cleared my throat, hesitating. "And that's… soon?"

"Just a few days away," she said, practically glowing as she glanced up. "I've got my entry confirmed and everything."

My stomach twisted, though I kept my face neutral. She had no idea what was at stake here. My father's plans were underway to buy out Vitello's mortgage from the bank—he'd already mentioned his intentions to bulldoze the place and replace it with one of his upscale restaurant brands. Annie was oblivious.

"Annie," I began slowly, watching her expression shift as I spoke, "I know you're excited, but don't you think you've got... a lot on your plate right now?"

She paused, one hand hovering over a package of pasta. "What do you mean?"

I took a breath, choosing my words carefully. "We're getting married in a few days. I mean, it's great that you're passionate about this competition, but maybe we should focus on... you know, the wedding?"

She gave me a half smile as if trying to mask the hurt. "Trent, it's just a competition. It doesn't mean I'm not focused on the wedding. I just thought... well, it's important to me."

I could feel her tension as she spoke, her enthusiasm dimming slightly, and I knew I'd touched a nerve. But the more I thought about it, the more frustrated I felt.

How could she be worrying about a cooking contest when we had so many other things to deal with?

"Important enough to neglect your responsibilities?" I asked, keeping my voice steady, though irritation was creeping in. "This is supposed to be about us, Annie. You and me, building a life together. A competition? That's… I don't know, that seems a little… off."

She pulled the cart forward, avoiding my gaze. "You know how much I love cooking, Trent. And this competition… it's a chance for me to prove something. And," she hesitated, "it could help Vitello's. I thought you'd be happy for me."

"It's not that I'm not happy," I said, though the words sounded less reassuring than I'd intended. "I just feel like maybe your priorities should be focused elsewhere right now. Don't you?"

She bit her lip, clearly frustrated, but I could see the determination in her eyes. "This isn't just a hobby for me, Trent. I thought you understood that."

Her words stung.

"Look," I tried, reaching for a compromise. "I get that this is important to you. I'm not trying to say it isn't. But wouldn't it make more sense to put this energy into the life we're going to share?"

Her expression shifted, her eyes softening

but with a hint of sadness. "I am, Trent. This competition isn't about choosing between cooking and our life together. It's just something I need to do."

The words hung in the air between us, creating a rift I hadn't expected.

As we reached the checkout line, I tried one last time. "Annie... can't this wait? Just until after the wedding?"

She turned to me, her face softened, but there was a firmness in her expression that left no room for negotiation. "I can't wait, Trent. This is happening. I need you to trust me. Can you do that?"

I opened my mouth to respond, but the words wouldn't come.

Trust her?

Sure, I wanted to. But when her dream felt so at odds with mine, how could I step aside and let it play out?

She took my silence as an answer and turned back to finish checking out, her movements efficient and focused. But the warmth between us, the excitement we'd once shared, felt like it had faded into the background, replaced by something I couldn't quite name.

Chapter Seventeen

Annie

When I walked into my tiny apartment, the last thing I expected was to be greeted by a full dinner spread… and an even fuller view of Jordan, bare-chested, barefoot, toes peeking from the cast, and leaning against my kitchen counter in a pair of low-slung jeans. I stopped short, one foot barely over the threshold, as I took it all in: the candles flickering on the table, the rich, comforting aroma of matzo ball soup filling the air, and then, of course, the sight of him.

My eyes did a quick, involuntary scan from his tousled hair all the way down to his bare feet.

Lord, help me.

It wasn't just that he looked good—it was that he looked so… at home. Here in my space, as if he was meant to be part of it all. And for one wild second, I imagined what it would be like if he were. If he was the one I came home to every night.

Which was, of course, absurd.

I had a fiancé. A dependable, proper fiancé who wore button-downs and knew how to pick out a decent wine based on the label and not what was on special in aisle seven. Trent was the man I was going to marry. Not Jordan. Jordan, with his bare feet and those damn jeans and the muscles that seemed to appear out of nowhere, like he'd somehow hit the gym since breaking his leg.

And yet, standing there, it was impossible not to feel the ridiculous, sudden warmth pooling low in my belly. Jordan had made dinner.

For me.

And Trent?

Well, I couldn't recall a single time he'd actually created something for me with his own hands. Anything Trent had ever given me came with a price tag with several zeros and a shiny designer label. I couldn't remember the last time he'd done something so... *genuine.*

Shaking myself out of the haze, I forced a laugh, determined to break the spell. "You know, most people start with flowers. You went straight for the matzo ball soup."

He grinned, though there was something softer in his gaze, something that made my heart do a traitorous little flip. "Figured you'd appreciate the direct approach."

I took a few steps further in, setting my bag down and trying to keep my eyes from wandering back to his abs. "Is that so? Well, you know me well, then."

He shrugged, glancing down at the pot simmering on the stove. "Thought you could use a night off. Figured a little homemade dinner might hit the spot."

The warmth from the stove wrapped around me like a hug, carrying the savory scent of chicken broth mingled with fresh dill and the faint nuttiness of matzo meal. It reminded me of the nights we used to spend experimenting in Granny's old, cramped kitchen back in Kansas, where we laughed too loud and argued over whether a pinch of salt meant his fingers or my fingers. The flickering candlelight cast golden hues across the table, softening the edges of the room in a way that felt almost too intimate.

I let my fingers brush the edge of the linen napkin Jordan had set out—real linen, not the paper ones I usually grabbed from the corner store. It was such a small, thoughtful detail. Yet it stirred something deep inside me. Back then, he'd been the one who insisted the presentation mattered, even when we were just cooking for ourselves. "Food deserves respect," he used to say. And looking at the effort he'd put into this meal, I realized how much that part of him hadn't changed.

I couldn't help but smile, though my

defenses were still up. "I didn't realize matzo ball soup was part of your repertoire. What, are you angling for my spot at Vitello's now?"

Jordan's face softened, and he let out a small chuckle, but there was something else in his eyes, a shadow from our past. "Annie, you know I'd never compete with you. Not then, not now."

The air between us shifted, the lightheartedness fading as the weight of our past settled over us. I leaned back against the counter, arms crossed, trying to hold on to my resolve.

"Really? Because last time, you didn't seem to mind taking first place over me," I shot back, unable to keep the bitterness out of my voice.

Jordan's face fell, and he took a slow, measured breath. "Annie... you know that wasn't my intention. I never wanted things to go down like that."

I felt my defenses rise even higher, memories of that night coming back in full force. I'd entered that competition ready to make my mark, only to watch Jordan, my supposed partner, overshadow me completely. It felt like betrayal, and I hadn't been able to shake that feeling since.

"Then what was your intention, Jordan? Because it sure didn't feel like you had my back. You went in, and you made it all about you. And I... I ended up feeling like a complete fool."

He ran a hand through his hair, frustration

flickering across his face. "Annie, I was young and stupid, and I thought... I thought we could share that win. I never realized how much it would hurt you. I just wanted us to succeed."

"By stepping on me in the process?" I shot back, hating how much anger was still wrapped up in the words. "You didn't think, Jordan. You just... went for it."

Jordan took a step toward me, his gaze intent. "I made a mistake. I didn't realize how much that moment mattered to you. But Annie, it was never about trying to outdo you. I was just... scared. Scared that if I didn't take that opportunity, I'd never get another chance."

His words stopped me cold. Fear. Not ambition. Not arrogance.

Fear.

It hit me harder than I expected, forcing me to confront a truth I'd been trying to bury since that night.

Hadn't I been scared, too? Terrified, even? The way my hands shook as I plated my dish, the late nights spent rehearsing recipes in my head, the constant voice whispering that I'd never measure up.

I clung to my anger like a shield, but now it felt less solid, more like smoke slipping through my fingers. Letting it go meant acknowledging that his mistake wasn't about me—it was about him. And if I admitted that, I'd have to face the fact that maybe I wasn't as blameless as I'd always told myself.

Jordan's restraint underscored the distance between the man he had been and the man standing in front of me. The boy I'd known might have leaned into this moment, let the unresolved tension pull us into something reckless. But this man? He stepped back. He held the line.

And damn him for that.

For making me see that growth didn't always come with a neat bow of forgiveness. For showing me he still had a piece of my heart and I had no idea what to do about it.

Chapter Eighteen

Jordan

The competition venue buzzed with energy as I approached, and I felt that familiar jolt of anticipation ripple through me. Even on crutches, with a leg still bruised and bound in a cast, I felt ready.

More than ready.

My eyes flicked to my watch, realizing I was cutting it close. The nerves prickled, but I brushed them aside. This was the Whisk It All competition, the ultimate culinary showdown I'd been eyeing for years. It felt like every step I took—even the awkward ones on crutches—was leading me toward something big.

The place was packed. I could see the other contestants milling around in their aprons and chef jackets, chatting or getting in the zone. Stainless steel prep tables glinted under the lights, shining like silver, and the air was thick with the scent of fresh herbs, ground spices, and a faint hint of nervous sweat. All around me, the excitement was contagious. This was it. This was my moment to prove what I could do.

With every bit of prep I'd done, every ingredient I'd tested and recipe I'd fine-tuned, I'd been building toward this. I couldn't deny the thrill, and though my leg throbbed with every step, it didn't matter. I was here. Crutches or not, I was ready to give it everything I had. My nerves were wound tight, but beneath them, the adrenaline was humming, pushing me forward.

I let out a slow breath, steadying myself. *Game face on,* I thought, squaring my shoulders as best I could with crutches. I'd worked too hard to let anything stand in my way. Today was going to be a turning point—I could feel it. And I was prepared to go all in.

As I hobbled over to the front desk, I took a moment to pull on my best "disarming" smile. After all, my predicament was far from typical, and I needed this check-in to go smoothly. The woman behind the desk looked efficient to the point of intimidating, her dark-rimmed glasses perched at the edge of her nose as she scanned through a thick roster of names.

"Hi, I'm Jordan Shaw," I began, leaning in a bit to make sure she could hear me over the hum of activity around us. "I'm a contestant—well, I'm *supposed* to be," I clarified, my smile widening as I gestured to the crutches. "Had a bit of an accident recently, and, uh… I seem to have misplaced my credentials in the shuffle."

She looked up, eyes narrowing as she scanned me from head to toe, taking in the crutches and cast. I kept my expression friendly, hoping she'd see the humor in the situation. "My name should be on the list," I added, tapping the roster with a hopeful smile. "I'm definitely supposed to be here."

She glanced back down at her paperwork, clearly unconvinced. "Mr. Shaw, I'm afraid all our contestants have already checked in," she said in a clipped tone. "Every slot has been confirmed. Are you sure you're on this list? Did you confirm by the due date?"

I felt my stomach tighten, but I kept my tone casual, forcing my smile to stay in place. "Well, sort of. I emailed explaining," I added, lifting the crutches for emphasis. "If you could just double-check…"

She sighed, adjusting her glasses as she rifled through the pages once more. I leaned in, silently willing my name to appear, refusing to believe that I'd somehow missed out on this after everything I'd been through. Nearby, a faint commotion at the check-in desk caught my attention—a staff member whispering hurriedly about a competitor being "in no condition to compete." I brushed it off, focused on making my case.

The coordinator looked up from her paperwork, and the skeptical look she leveled at me was enough to make me straighten on my crutches, nerves prickling.

"Mr. Shaw," she said with a firm tone, "I understand your situation, but all the slots for today's competition have been filled. There's simply no room for additional contestants." She closed the roster with an air of finality, as if she'd said all there was to say.

A pang of disbelief shot through me, settling in my gut like a rock. This had to be a mistake. "Are you sure?" I managed, doing my best to keep my voice steady despite the frustration building beneath the surface. "Help a guy out, huh?"

The coordinator's eyes narrowed slightly, her lips pressing into a thin line as if she'd heard every excuse under the sun. "I double-checked, Mr. Shaw. There's no entry under your name. We have a strict policy, and all slots were confirmed and filled."

I swallowed hard, trying to keep the irritation at bay. A pulse of frustration tightened my grip on the crutches. I'd worked so hard, prepared meticulously, and now, because of some error, I was being shut out. "I know this must seem… unorthodox," I said, my voice tight with a

139

forced calm, "but my name has to be there. Maybe it was a glitch, an oversight? Isn't there any way you can verify?"

She cleared her throat, clearly not amused by my persistence. "Mr. Shaw, I've been coordinating this competition for over a decade. We have no oversights," she replied matter-of-factly. "Now, I'm very sorry for your situation, but the list is final."

I felt a flush of heat climb up my neck as I struggled to maintain composure, the injustice of it all making my chest tighten. This was supposed to be my chance, and I couldn't believe it was slipping through my fingers.

I took a deep breath, trying to keep my cool. "I understand this is a tightly run competition," I began, keeping my tone polite but firm. "But I'm telling you, I belong on that list. This competition is everything I've been working toward."

The coordinator's gaze didn't soften, and she simply gave a small, sympathetic shake of her head. "I appreciate your enthusiasm, Mr. Shaw," she said, her voice clipped but professional, "but as I mentioned, all the slots were filled. There's no record of your name on this list."

"Can you check one more time?" I asked, trying to keep the desperation from my voice. "It's got to be there. The email explained everything.

Maybe someone accidentally moved my name, or maybe it's filed under a different spelling or something. I mean, mistakes happen, right?"

She looked at me like I was a kid begging for extra credit after failing the final. "This isn't a matter of a spelling error, Mr. Shaw. We have a full roster. Every participant has checked in. Our policy is clear—only those with confirmed entries may compete."

My patience was wearing thin, and I could feel a bead of frustration trickling down my spine. I'd fought so hard to make it to this point, even through the accident and the crutches, and now I was being told, in no uncertain terms, that my spot didn't exist? It was almost surreal.

"Can I see the list?" I sighed.

She raised an eyebrow. "I'm sorry, but without credentials or a confirmed place, there's nothing I can do."

Each word felt like a nail in the coffin.

I opened my mouth, about to argue my case further, when a flash of movement by the entrance caught my eye. My words stalled as I recognized that auburn hair, those familiar features—Annie. She was scanning the room with a look of wide-eyed excitement. Her face practically glowed with anticipation. And as if that wasn't shocking enough, there was one unmistakable detail around her neck: a competition lanyard.

Everything clicked into place in an instant, my surprise morphing into a simmering frustration that ran straight through me. I could hardly believe it.

She took my spot.

I stared, watching her float through the room as if she belonged there, completely oblivious to my presence and the chaos she'd just caused. She seemed so comfortable, looking for all the world as if she deserved that spot.

This was an ambush.

The coordinator, still standing behind me, cleared her throat, probably preparing to dismiss me again, but I barely heard her. My focus was locked on Annie.

A slow heat built in my chest as I followed her with my eyes, noting the way she paused, looking around the venue with admiration. Did she think this was a harmless, victimless little scheme? That I wouldn't show up and just let her waltz in on my hard work?

My jaw tightened as I gripped my crutches, feeling that initial shock melt away, leaving only frustration and, if I was honest, a bit of betrayal. Annie had snagged my spot, my shot at finally proving myself. And for what?

I watched Annie move through the room, my chance hanging around her neck like a trophy, as if she belonged here more than I did.

I tightened my grip on the crutches, hobbling toward her with a determination that only anger can fuel. My leg throbbed with each step, but I ignored it, too focused on the rising frustration in my chest. I kept my voice low as I approached her, not wanting to make a scene, though every part of me wanted to call her out for all to hear.

"Annie," I said sharply, making her turn around. Her eyes widened as she saw me, caught completely off guard. There was a brief flicker of guilt—maybe even panic—in her expression before she attempted a nervous smile.

"Jordan... hey! I didn't expect you to be here," she said, her tone overly casual, as if we'd run into each other at the grocery store instead of the competition I'd trained months for.

I didn't bother with pleasantries.

"You found my application." My voice was barely above a whisper, but the intensity made her flinch. I held her gaze, watching her face shift as she searched for an answer, some excuse that could smooth over the fact that she'd blindsided me like this. "You took my spot."

Annie glanced down, clutching the lanyard around her neck before meeting my eyes again. "Look, Jordan, I... I can explain," she started, her voice wavering slightly. But I could tell she hadn't planned on being confronted—hadn't expected to be caught. And that realization only made me angrier.

"Explain? You're wearing the last entry badge, Annie," I hissed, forcing myself to keep my tone low.

She shifted uncomfortably, a flash of guilt crossing her face. "I… well, I figured—"

"You figured what?" I interrupted, unwilling to let her talk her way out of this. "That I wouldn't notice? That I'd just skip out on my chance at something as big as this?" I felt my hands tighten around the crutches as I waited, the silence between us as tense as a taut wire.

My jaw tightened, the initial shock hardening into anger. Annie had stolen my spot—my chance to prove myself. For what?

Revenge?

The thing was, it wasn't just my opportunity on the line—it was hers, too. Whether she realized it, I wasn't here just for me. I had come to help her save Vitello's, even if I couldn't bring myself to tell her.

If I failed, it wouldn't just be my pride bruised; it would be another mark against everything I'd ever done to make things right between us. She didn't know that, though. And if she did, would it even matter?

Either way, the woman in front of me felt like a stranger.

She glanced at the lanyard, then back at me, her smile faltering. "Look, Jordan, I... I can explain." Her voice wavered, and she took a small step back, as though creating space would soften the confrontation.

"Explain?" I hissed.

Her expression wavered, a war of emotions playing across her face — guilt, defiance, desperation. Finally, she squared her shoulders, her chin lifting just slightly. "You don't understand," she said, her tone clipped. "This was important. More important than you realize."

My stomach tightened at her evasiveness. "Important?" I said, incredulous. "Important enough to steal my spot?"

She looked away, her fingers curling nervously around the lanyard. "I didn't steal anything," she said, her voice quieter but tinged with a defensive edge. "The application was there, and I... borrowed it. I thought maybe..."

"You thought what?" I interrupted, my voice rising.

Her jaw tightened, and she met my gaze, her expression a mix of defiance and something rawer, harder to pin down. "I thought you'd understand," she said finally, her voice barely above a whisper. "I thought you, of all people, would get it."

She looked away, her grip tightening on the

lanyard as her shoulders sagged. For a moment, it looked like she was debating whether to say something, her lips pressing together before parting again. "Do you think this was easy for me?" she murmured, barely loud enough for me to hear.

Her gaze darted past me, fixing on some indeterminate spot in the crowd, as if facing me directly was too much. "I know how this looks. I know what you're thinking. But I didn't have another option." Her voice wavered, like the words were dragging something heavier behind them. "This wasn't about trying to hurt you. It was…" she trailed off, her brows knitting together, and for a second, it seemed like she was wrestling with whatever she couldn't bring herself to say. Her gaze faltered, and for a moment, she looked down at the lanyard, her fingers fidgeting with the edge.

"You think I wanted to do this?" she murmured, almost too quietly to hear. Her voice wavered, thick with something that sounded too much like regret. "I didn't plan for it to go this way, Jordan. But… it's not as simple as you think." She swallowed hard, her shoulders sagging as though the weight of her actions was finally catching up to her. "If there had been another way…" Her voice trailed off, and she shook her head, unable to finish the thought.

The defiance in her expression flickered, replaced by something closer to guilt — or maybe regret. "You've always had this way of making it look so easy," she said, her tone softening, almost bitter. "You show up, and things just… happen for you. But for me? It's never been like that."

She swallowed hard, her hands curling into fists. "This wasn't a choice, Jordan. Not really. It was survival. And if you can't see that…" She shook her head, the defiance returning as she blinked hard, as if willing herself not to falter any further. "Then maybe you don't know me as well as you think."

Her words stopped me cold, confusion threading through my frustration.

But I do know you, Annie.

That's the whole reason I was here. But I couldn't say it aloud. I couldn't push harder, couldn't let the truth spill out.

I wasn't here just to win.

I'm here for you.

And yet, the way she looked at me — like I was the obstacle, not the ally — made my chest hurt. She didn't know what I was risking for her, and I wasn't brave enough to tell her.

Annie stammered, her cheeks flushed, clearly scrambling for words. "Jordan, I… I didn't plan for it to go down like this," she started, her voice wavering. She glanced down, tugging nervously at the lanyard before looking back up at me. "I know how it looks, but I needed this opportunity. You have to understand. I didn't mean to hurt you."

Her words barely registered past the frustration pounding in my head. Needed this opportunity? Didn't mean to hurt me? It sounded like she was trying to rationalize what she'd done without really owning up to it.

Ouch. Hi, Pot. I'd like you to meet Kettle.

"Annie, do you even hear yourself?" I asked, my jaw tight as I fought to keep my voice steady. "You took something that didn't belong to you."

She winced, but held her ground. "Now, you know how it feels."

The accusation hit like a punch to the gut. I opened my mouth to argue, but the words stuck, a flash of old memories breaking through my frustration. She would always hold them against me—the last competition, the one where I took first place while she was left in my shadow. I'd never meant for it to end up like that, and I'd apologized a dozen times, but here it was, boiling to the surface all over again.

"You know that was different," I managed, though even I could hear the wavering in my voice.

"Was it?" she shot back, her voice heated.

"Because from where I'm standing, it looks like I'm finally giving you a taste of your own medicine."

Her words hit harder than I wanted to admit. She was digging up the past, wielding it like a weapon, and it stung. I knew exactly what she meant — the last competition we'd entered together, when I'd won, and she'd walked away feeling sidelined, like she'd been nothing more than my warm-up act. It wasn't what I'd intended. I'd tried to apologize back then, tried to explain, but she'd clearly held onto that bitterness.

Her jaw clenched, her eyes blazing. "I'm doing what I have to, Jordan," she replied, voice sharp. "And maybe it's time you felt what it's like to have your dreams crushed."

But it's supposed to be our dream.

I wanted to scream it from the rooftops.

I shook my head, anger flaring up again. "I hope it's worth it, Annie. I really do."

Our voices stayed low, but the intensity between us was anything but. "I didn't have a choice, Jordan," Annie insisted, her jaw set in that stubborn way I knew too well.

The words slipped out, harsh and defensive, before I could stop myself. "At least I had a good reason."

I couldn't take it anymore. The words, the accusations, the reminder of how tangled up we'd become over the years. It felt like trying to rebuild something on a foundation that had cracked beyond repair. Without another word, I turned on my crutches and started hobbling away, each step harder than it needed to be, as frustration burned through me. I could feel Annie's gaze on my back, heavy with all the things she hadn't said, but I didn't stop. I just kept moving, the desire to put as much distance between us as possible overriding everything else.

Under my breath, I muttered, "I hope you get everything you deserve," the words dripping with a mix of resentment and finality. I wanted her to know that I wouldn't just forgive this, wouldn't let her push me out so easily. But as the words settled in the air, a hollow ache spread through my chest. Vindicated or not, it was impossible to ignore the sense of loss creeping in, a bitter reminder of what we'd once had—and had lost all over again.

The chilly air outside hit me hard as I stepped out of the venue, inhaling deeply and letting it clear my head. I needed it. My mind was a mess, replaying every word Annie and I had just thrown at each other. The anger, the betrayal—it all sat like a weight on my chest, tightening with each breath. I knew I had two options: go back in there and keep fighting for my place or just... walk away. Maybe I'd find another opportunity someday, a different competition with a fresh start, untainted by this mess. But that wasn't guaranteed and leaving now felt like giving up on everything I'd worked so hard for.

As I lifted my hand to hail a cab, disappointment washed over me in waves. The idea of leaving without even trying, after all I'd sacrificed to be here, felt unbearable. I deserved my shot, too.

Just as my resolve began to weaken, I heard footsteps approaching quickly. I turned and saw the competition coordinator, slightly out of breath, a look of urgency on her face.

"Mr. Shaw!" the coordinator called out, her voice sharp enough to cut through my haze of frustration. I turned, startled, as she jogged toward me, her clipboard clutched tightly and her expression unusually flustered. "I'm glad I caught you."

Her words carried an urgency that sent a jolt through me. She caught her breath, her eyes scanning me as if evaluating whether I could even compete in my current state. "One competitor had to drop out—food poisoning, if you can believe it. We've got a last-minute opening," she said quickly, barely pausing before adding, "If you still want it, the spot's yours."

For a moment, all I could do was stare at her, the weight of the day's events pressing against the possibility she was offering me. It felt impossible—like fate had twisted itself into a pretzel just to give me this one last shot.

She glanced at her watch, her tone shifting to something more urgent. "But I need your answer now, Mr. Shaw. We're about to start prep. If you're in, you'll need to move fast."

The world seemed to tilt for a second as I processed her words. After everything—Annie's betrayal, the coordinator's earlier dismissal, the crushing disappointment of being turned away—this felt like a lifeline I hadn't dared hope for. My heart thudded against my ribs as I gripped my crutches tighter. This was it. My chance.

"Yes," I said, my voice steady despite the adrenaline pumping through me. "I'll take it."

Her lips tightened into something between relief and resolve. "Good. Follow me—now."

As I hobbled back toward the venue, a surge of energy hit me, sharper and more focused than before. This was my moment, and I was ready to prove, once and for all, that I deserved it. Annie could do whatever she wanted. I was back in the game.

Here we go again.

Chapter Nineteen

Trent

I stepped into the grand foyer of my parents' estate, feeling the weight of their expectations settle on my shoulders. Everything was perfectly arranged, guests floating around the room with drinks in hand, their laughter and low voices blending into a practiced symphony of elegance. The rehearsal dinner was as seamless as my parents would expect—a perfect display of wealth and tradition.

Then I spotted Annie across the room, standing with Aunt Margaret, her smile a little too tight, her laugh just a touch too loud. She wasn't herself here, and I could feel it in every stiff movement, every cautious glance. Annie wasn't used to this world of polished façades and quiet judgment, and it showed. But then again, that was part of what I loved about her—she didn't belong here, not really, and maybe that was why I found her so magnetic in the first place.

My mind drifted to the day we wandered

through the farmer's market downtown. She'd dragged me to a stall selling wildflowers, then charmed the older woman running it by naming every flower in the bouquet—correctly. The woman had laughed and told her she had a knack for it, and Annie had beamed as if she'd won the lottery. Then she'd plucked a stray daisy from the bunch and tucked it behind my ear with an impish grin, declaring me "the prettiest Parker at the market." I'd felt ridiculous, but her joy was infectious. She had that way about her—pulling you into her orbit, making everything feel a little lighter, a little brighter.

Here, though, she seemed dimmed, like someone had turned down the light inside her. She wasn't darting around the room with her usual energy; instead, she was carefully navigating conversations, visibly trying to measure up to the unspoken standards of this crowd. I spotted her nodding along as Aunt Margaret prattled on about her recent trip to Provence, and I could see the effort it took for Annie to keep her face neutral, her responses polite. She wasn't flourishing—she was floundering.

I wanted to pull her aside, tell her she didn't need to try so hard, that her natural charm was enough. But then, that wasn't entirely true, was it? Not here. Not with these people. I hated how much it mattered, but it did. She'd have to fit in, somehow. This was my world — our world, if she wanted it — and she'd need to find her place in it.

Still, I couldn't help but wish that the Annie with the wildflowers and the daisy behind her ear would make an appearance. That Annie was unstoppable. But this Annie — tense, uncertain, trying so hard to be someone she wasn't — this wasn't her. And it wasn't what I wanted for her, either.

As I watched, she reached for a champagne flute from a passing tray, her eyes on Aunt Margaret instead of her hand. Her fingers brushed the edge of another glass, nearly sending it flying. She caught it before it crashed to the floor, but not before it splashed Dom Perignon all over Aunt Margaret's dress. Annie's cheeks flushed pink as she glanced apologetically at my aunt.

"Oh! I'm so sorry. That's not Shantung, is it?" She dabbed hopelessly at the dress with a cocktail napkin. Aunt Margaret looked slightly scandalized, as if she'd just watched a child nearly knock over a priceless vase. Annie laughed it off, but I could tell she was mortified.

A part of me found it charming — her refreshing roughness against all this polish. But I also couldn't help thinking that, with time, she'd have to learn to move a little more carefully.

I leaned against a pillar, watching Annie attempt to mingle with my family and their crowd. She was trying—God, was she trying—with that wide smile plastered on, making polite small talk and nodding. The scene was almost endearing. She was doing her best, I supposed, but it was obvious she didn't quite belong here. I could see it in the way she stumbled through conversations about country club galas and European ski trips, her eyes glazing over whenever someone mentioned the Hamptons.

Part of me felt a stab of annoyance, thinking how much easier this would all be if she'd just… fit in. These weren't complicated conversations, really, just the expected pleasantries of people with a certain standard. I found myself silently willing her to ease up, to tone down some of that small-town charm and realize she was part of something bigger now.

For a second, I considered going over, maybe giving her a few pointers on how to carry herself with a bit more polish. But I stopped myself. She'd have to learn eventually—especially if she was going to stand by my side in this world. This wasn't just a cute little neighborhood hangout like Vitello's. This was my family's circle, people who would make up her clientele once we got the new restaurant going.

Once we were married, she'd understand.

She'd settle down, smooth out those rough edges, and start living up to the Parker name. She was adaptable enough, surely. This little rough-around-the-edges vibe she had would fade in time, and maybe she'd even be grateful for what I was bringing her into.

I sighed. Bored. The evening had barely started, and I already felt like I'd been navigating the niceties for hours. Everywhere I turned, it was more handshakes, polite smiles, and stale jokes, the same hollow compliments cycling through the air. I moved through the grand foyer, stopping when necessary, nodding to second cousins and family friends whose names I could barely remember.

"Trent, my boy! I hear you're finally settling down!" Uncle Ray caught me with a clap on the shoulder, his grip too firm, his drink sloshing slightly as he leaned in close. "Didn't think you'd ever tie the knot!"

I forced a laugh, trying to shrug it off. "Guess the right merger finally came along."

Ray laughed, too, like I'd cracked the most original joke in the world. "Smart man, smart man," he said, giving my shoulder one last squeeze before turning his attention back to his drink.

I moved on, dodging a few more clusters of guests until I was pulled into yet another conversation, this time with Great-Uncle Herbert.

"So, Trent, this little restaurant venture of yours," Herbert began, waving a hand like it was some passing whim. "Your father tells me it's a real project, hmm? Big plans for this place, I hear."

I nodded, keeping my tone casual. "We're looking to make it something special, yes. Something that could really elevate the area. God knows it needs it."

Uncle Herbert chuckled, his bushy eyebrows waggling. "You're a Parker, all right. Always reaching for the stars, eh?"

I nodded, giving him a tight smile. I knew what he meant. "Reaching for the stars" in my family meant hitting our benchmarks and elevating our brand. It was all anyone here seemed to care about.

Just as I was about to edge my way out, I spotted my mother striding toward me, her expression as polished as the chandelier glinting above her. She gave a short, approving nod to Herbert before turning to me, a familiar pinched look crossing her face.

"Where is your father?" she asked, her voice just low enough for me to hear but still holding that unmistakable edge. Her gaze swept across the room, pausing briefly on Annie, who was now talking to Great-Aunt Lila with a bit too much enthusiasm. I caught the faintest purse of my mother's lips.

"And Trent, darling, about Annie..." She let the sentence hang, the word itself wrapped in a layer of barely veiled distaste. "She's...lovely, of course. But are you certain she's ready for this life? I worry she's...well, you know."

I kept my tone even, nodding. "She'll adjust, Mom. Just give her time."

Mom sighed, still eyeing Annie with a doubtful look. "I certainly hope so. We're giving you a lot of responsibility with this..." She broke off, her eyes narrowing as she scanned the room. "Speaking of we... where *is* your father? He should be out here mingling with the guests, making sure everyone feels attended to. What must they think, him hiding away like this?"

I knew that tone all too well—my mother's barely restrained irritation, something she saved for occasions like these. "I'll go find him," I offered, and with a curt nod, she glided off to greet another group.

With a quick excuse to Uncle Herbert, I slipped out of the main room, sidestepping more guests and weaving through the house toward the study. The last thing I wanted was a lecture from my mother about family presence and appearances.

The study was dimly lit, the TV casting a faint blue glow across the walls. Sure enough, there was my father, seated in his leather armchair, his posture rigid as he stared at the screen. His jaw was set, lips pressed in a firm line that told me he wasn't exactly in the best of moods.

I cleared my throat. "Dad?"

He didn't even look up, his eyes fixed on the muted news channel. Finally, he gave me a sidelong glance. "So, you're finally here," he muttered, gaze drifting back to the screen. "Have you charmed the crowd yet? Or are they all still wondering why we're here?"

I forced a smile, keeping my tone light. "Just doing the rounds. You know how it is."

He snorted, his gaze still on the TV. "Yes, well, *some* of us know how to keep up appearances." His voice was low and pointed, each word sharp. He pointed his whiskey glass at the television where Annie was standing mighty chummy next to an extremely good-looking man.

My father eyed my surprised look with suspicion as he sipped his liquor. "You know who this bozo is?"

"I, um…"

My father's eyes narrowed to thin slits. *Yeah. Wrong answer.*

He clunked his heavy crystal glass on the end table. "That," he pointed at the screen where the would-be Abercrombie & Fitch model grinned, "is a potential roadblock to our plan. Seems like she and this... mutt were once an item. And they're competing in the Whisk It All competition? How is it you knew nothing about it?"

"I...I..."

My father shook his head. "Nope. No eyes. That's exactly why you didn't see what's going on right under your nose, goddammit!"

I straightened. "Annie's committed, Dad. She knows what's expected of her," I replied, forcing my voice to sound resolute. But the moment the words left my mouth, I realized just how empty they sounded.

My father's lip curled, barely concealing his disdain. "Let's hope so. We can't afford for you to be distracted by some girl playing Easy Bake Oven with a crush from her past. If she can't toe the line, I suggest you start reconsidering your options. Because a woman too busy pining after another man isn't exactly Parker wife material."

I clenched my jaw, frustration and anger twisting through me. "She'll do what she's told."

He raised an eyebrow, his gaze sharp, but he looked almost...satisfied. "Good. Because when I tear that dump down the day after Valentine's, I want her ready to run my restaurant."

A flicker of movement caught my attention at the door. I turned, catching sight of the door barely cracked open—and there was Annie, standing half in the shadows, her eyes wide and her hand clamped over her mouth, her face ashen as she took a shaky breath.

Chapter Twenty

Annie

The moment I stepped into the entryway of Trent's parents' estate, it was like I'd wandered onto the set of Downton Abbey. Marble floors polished to a mirror shine, massive chandeliers glinting above, walls decorated with artwork that looked…well, intimidatingly expensive. It was breathtaking, yes, but it didn't exactly scream "welcome" or "family," and it certainly didn't look like a place you'd ever want to spill a glass of red wine.

I pasted on a polite smile and tried to push down the growing feeling that I was playing a tiny part in a very large theater production. Everything around me sparkled and gleamed, a flawless surface that I definitely didn't feel a part of. In fact, I felt more like the accidental guest—here by invitation, maybe, but with no idea how I was supposed to fit in.

"Annie! My dear, you must be the famous fiancée," boomed a voice to my left. I turned to see a silver-haired man I'd never met, grinning as if he'd known me my whole life.

"That's me," I replied, forcing my voice to sound upbeat. "Well, fiancée anyway . Not sure about the famous part." I gave a quick, awkward laugh, hoping against hope he wasn't referring to the sticky sound bite from earlier today. I wondered if anyone here caught the coverage of the Whisk It All opening festivities.

Does Fox News cover cooking shows?

"Well, don't be shy, sweetheart," he said, patting me on the shoulder a little too hard. "We've all been waiting to meet you."

And with that, I was passed along, greeted and patted, complimented and questioned by Trent's extended family and friends. I felt like show-and-tell on the first day of kindergarten. I smiled so much my face hurt, I wondered if anyone could see through me, see how out of place I felt. A familiar figure across the room caught my eye — Trent, chatting with a small group, looking polished and relaxed, blending seamlessly into the scene.

He made it look so easy!

I floated from one conversation to the next, each one leaving me more adrift than before. It felt like I'd wandered into an exclusive seminar on topics I'd never imagined people actually discussed outside of movies.

"Oh, yes," a tall man with slicked-back hair

was saying as I approached. "We doubled our shares in Jannerson, Ltd. Right before the market shifted. Paid for the Aspen house." He laughed, noticing me. "What about you, Annie? Play the market at all?"

"Uh… only for produce," I replied, smiling tightly. "If tomatoes are on sale, I'm all over it."

The laughter was polite but faint, and the group quickly moved on, diving back into their stories of real estate and hedge funds.

A woman in a floor-length gown smiled at me, though the look in her eye felt a bit too curious. "You're the chef, yes? How fascinating," she cooed. "And do you plan on working at that little restaurant *after* the wedding? Or will you start a family right away?"

"Oh, well, I'm… still working that out," I said, trying to keep my tone light.

"How charming," she murmured, clearly uninterested, already glancing over my shoulder in search of a more interesting conversation.

Then came Great-Uncle Herbert, who cleared his throat as he regarded me with a polite but vacant look. "So, tell me, what made you go with cooking?" He tilted his head thoughtfully, as if discussing an unusual hobby. "Surely you could have chosen something… I don't know, more practical?"

I forced a smile, tucking a stray hair behind

my ear. "I don't know. I think eating is pretty practical," I replied, hoping he might at least appreciate the sentiment. But his nod was already on its way out, his focus drifting back to stocks or bonds or whatever else rich uncles concerned themselves with.

With each polite, disinterested question, I felt more like a novelty than an actual part of this gathering, as though I were here on a trial run. I kept glancing at Trent across the room, trying to gauge if he noticed. He looked perfectly at ease, laughing at something his uncle said, looking every inch the perfect fit in this room of pressed suits and pearls. I wondered if he understood exactly how much of a square peg he was asking me to become.

As I wandered through the room, trying to ignore the conversations about stocks and vacation homes, I glimpsed myself in an enormous gilded mirror mounted on the far wall. For a moment, I didn't recognize the woman staring back at me. My hair was swept up in an elaborate twist, pinned into submission, and my dress—a designer loan from Trent's mother, something tasteful, timeless, and entirely *not me*—hugged my frame like it was trying to reshape me. The person reflected felt more like a character I was trying to play, someone I didn't really know.

A pang of unease crept up, and I fought to

push it down. I'd come here tonight to celebrate the future, to support Trent and our impending life together. And yet…standing here, I felt like an intruder, dressed in borrowed finery, circling a world I'd never dreamed of being part of. I smoothed down my dress, adjusting a wayward curl, trying to remind myself that this was just another chapter, another layer of experience.

But as I looked around at the impeccably dressed crowd, the small voice inside — the one that's always grounded me, the one that knows who I am and what I love — grew louder. I'd never cared about status or designer labels. I'd grown up around people who knew my name — Granny McGowan, Louie, Curtis…

… *Jordan*.

People who preferred genuine conversations to social posturing. My life was rooted in community, in food, in family, not in being some carefully groomed accessory.

A feeling settled over me — a realization, really. Being here, part of Trent's world, meant I'd have to compromise pieces of myself that I wasn't ready to let go of. The more I tried to smooth myself into the image of the perfect fiancée, the more I felt like I was losing touch with the person I'd always been. And the question that had been quietly growing in the back of my mind felt urgent: Was I even supposed to fit into this world?

I needed to get out of here.

I spun away from the mirror, only to collide straight into Aunt Lydia, who clutched a crystal flute of Dom Pérignon.

I smashed right into her.

Time seemed to slow as the golden champagne splashed into the air, arcing toward Aunt Lydia's pristine shantung dress—a pale, luxurious fabric that seemed to gleam under the chandelier light. The champagne hit her in the center of her bodice, spreading out like a blossoming golden stain. The glass sailed toward the Italian marble floor, but I snagged it in the nick of time. But the victory was hollow.

"Oh! Oh my!" Aunt Lydia gasped, clutching at the fabric as if she could will it dry. Her face twisted into a polite mask, though the distaste behind her pinched smile was unmistakable. She dabbed at the dress with a perfectly manicured hand, looking less horrified by the stain and more as if she were suppressing the urge to recoil from *me*.

"Oh, I'm—I'm so sorry!" I stammered, hands flying to my mouth. "I didn't see you there—I just—"

"Clearly," Aunt Lydia interrupted. Her voice was tight, refined, laced with just enough icy restraint to make sure I knew exactly how she felt. I dabbed futilely at the damp silk with a cocktail napkin. Around us, guests murmured, their disapproving glances flicking over me as if I were some untrained puppy let loose in a glass menagerie. I could feel the weight of their judgment pressing in, making my cheeks burn.

A lady nearby leaned in, whispering behind a bejeweled hand to the woman next to her. The words were inaudible, but their looks weren't — raised brows, tight smiles, glances that silently conveyed *who let her in here?*

"I can pay for the dry cleaning," I offered, my voice too bright, too high-pitched, clinging to some desperate attempt to make it right. Aunt Lydia gave me a brittle smile that hardly contained an eye roll — her patience stretched beyond its limits.

"Yes…well," she said, her eyes cold. "I suppose these things…happen." She turned away, and as she walked off, heads turned with her, leaving me standing alone in a bubble of embarrassment. I wanted to shrink into the floor, but there was no escaping the judging stares, the muttered asides, or the uncomfortable realization that, to them, I was just a clumsy outsider.

The embarrassment from the champagne spill was still burning on my cheeks, and every attempt to find something — *anything* — familiar in the room only amplified the feeling. Heads still turned my way now and then, no doubt whispering about Trent's clumsy fiancée, and I could feel the weight of their polite judgment pressing down on me. My skin felt hot, my throat tight, and before I knew it, I was making a quick, quiet beeline for the nearest escape route.

I slipped into a powder room down the hall and closed the door behind me, letting out a shaky breath. The muted hum of conversation on the other side of the door was finally muffled, and for a moment, I allowed myself to just *be*. The quiet calm of the space, though still dressed in marble and gold leaf, felt like a retreat, if only because no one was watching.

I swallowed hard, pressing my hands to the cool edge of the sink, willing myself to calm down. *What was I even doing here?* This wasn't my world, and I was kidding myself to think that I could fit in. The further I ventured into Trent's life, the more I felt like I was leaving pieces of myself behind. And, standing here in a room that reflected a stranger's face, I realized just how completely, utterly alone I felt.

"I wish Jordan was here."

The out loud words caught me off guard, making me swallow hard. I *did* wish Jordan was here, not to sweep in and rescue me, but just to be...himself. His presence always made things feel less heavy, less complicated. He would have seen the humor in the champagne mishap with Aunt

Lydia and probably would've leaned in with some offhand joke that'd have me laughing instead of standing here, feeling like the odd puzzle piece forced into the wrong place.

It was strange, really, because Trent was the one I was supposed to be marrying, yet right now, it was Jordan's face, his affable grin and comforting humor, that came to mind. The thought of him grounded me, pulling me back to who I really was.

Even if I was furious with him.

I shook my head, pushing the thought aside, but a wistful ache lingered. I'd never felt so alone, so isolated from myself. The irony was, here I was, trying to fit into Trent's world, while a part of me couldn't stop wishing Jordan was here to pull me right back out of it.

I gripped the vanity, giving my reflection the kind of pep talk I hoped wouldn't sound desperate. "All right, Annie. You are a smart, capable woman. You can handle this. It's just a rehearsal dinner, not a G4 Summit." I forced a smile, hoping it looked more like confidence and less like I was bracing for impact.

But my reflection didn't seem convinced, so I pushed harder. "Besides, it's not like you haven't survived worse. Remember that dinner rush when the oven doors jammed shut, the stove went cold, and the only thing working was the temperamental fryer? You pulled through, even if it meant finishing pasta with a ladle of oil from the fries. If you can handle that chaos, you can handle Trent's family and their," I looked around at the ostentatious opulence of the room, "their monogrammed toilet paper."

I smoothed my dress and straightened my posture. "You've got this, Annie. You're not just a chef. You're a culinary warrior. You may be a disaster in heels, but I will *not* hide in this bathroom all night." With one last steadying breath, I pushed myself out the door, ready to face anything high-society could dish out.

I just hoped it didn't give me indigestion.

Chapter Twenty-One

Annie

I slipped out of the bathroom, taking a deep breath as I fixed my hair. With one last tug on my hem and a plastered-on smile, I was ready to dive back into the polished lion's den.

"Showtime," I whispered to myself, hoping my voice sounded a lot steadier than I felt.

The murmur of voices echoed down the grand hallway, but one voice stood out—Trent's, low and measured. Relief flooded over me. Finally, someone who could anchor me in all this chaos. I turned, heading toward the sound, preparing to slip in beside him and breathe a little easier. But as I approached, I caught his father's voice, rough and irritated, slicing through the air like a blade.

"That," he said, slamming his crystal glass on a side table, "is a potential roadblock to our plan." His voice dripped with disdain. "Seems like she and this…mutt were once an item. How is it you knew nothing about it?"

Trent stammered, "I…I…"

"Nope. No eyes. That's exactly why you didn't see what's going on right under your nose, goddammit!" His father's tone sharpened, and I froze, suddenly grateful for the shadows in the hall.

I heard Trent straighten, his voice stiff and tense. "Annie's committed, Dad. She knows what's expected of her." But his tone rang hollow, like even he didn't believe his words.

His father gave a derisive laugh. "Let's hope so. We can't afford for you to be distracted by some girl playing Easy Bake Oven with a crush from her past. If she can't toe the line, I suggest you start reconsidering your options. Because a woman too busy pining after another man isn't exactly Parker wife material."

Silence filled the air, thick and heavy. Then Trent spoke, his voice colder than I'd ever heard. "She'll do what she's told."

"Good." His father's tone softened, like he'd finally gotten what he wanted. "Because when I tear that dump down the day after Valentine's, I want her ready to run my restaurant."

My breath froze, every word echoing in my mind like a brutal, steady beat.

Tearing down Vitello's… the day after Valentine's.

They were planning to demolish the restaurant, the place that had been my second home, my sanctuary.

My hands shook, my pulse roaring in my ears. Trent, the man I was supposed to marry, had known about this? And he just…stood there, promising I'd "do what I was told." My heart twisted painfully, a swell of disbelief mingling with fury.

I took a shaky step back, feeling the sting of tears pressing against my eyes, and then — too late — I heard my own gasp, the sound a giveaway in the heavy silence of the hall. Trent's head jerked up, his gaze locking with mine, alarm flashing in his eyes. "Annie…"

But I couldn't hear another word. Before he could move, I spun and bolted, my mind racing with too many thoughts to process, and one word ringing in my ears: *betrayal.* He had kept this from me, let me believe we were building a life together while he stood by as they plotted to destroy the one place that mattered to me.

I stumbled through the crowd, pushing past the sea of silk and jewels. People turned in surprise, catching only a blur of me rushing by. My only thought was escape — I had to get out, to breathe, away from all the fake smiles and soulless conversations that made up Trent's world.

"Annie?" someone called, but I ignored

them, moving faster, barely noticing the way my hands clenched into fists. Vitello's was going to be erased. The restaurant that Louie had poured his life into, that had taken me in as more than just a chef — it was all just a line item to these people.

I stumbled outside, the cool night air hitting me like a slap. But it did nothing to clear the whirlwind inside. The weight of Trent's betrayal crashed down, harsh and relentless, leaving me breathless. I'd believed, really believed, that I'd found someone who understood me, who didn't just tolerate my dreams but celebrated them. Someone who knew what Vitello's meant, not only to me but to the community it had been part of for decades. I thought I'd found a partner — someone who didn't just support my passion but saw it as something real, valuable.

But all of that had been a lie.

To Trent, Vitello's was just another rundown piece of property waiting to be gutted and replaced with gleaming countertops and stainless steel appliances, a convenient addition to the Parker empire. All those late-night talks we'd had, where I'd rambled on about my goals and love for the restaurant, they were nothing but background noise to him. He hadn't cared at all.

My stomach twisted painfully. Every look, every promise, every quiet "I get it" from him had been empty, hollow. The truth hit me hard: Trent didn't care about what I wanted or who I was. He only cared that I looked the part, that I could fit into his world—just another glossy piece in the life he and his family had so neatly assembled.

And then there was Vitello's. Louie's pride and joy, the place where I'd honed my skills, built friendships, and found a second family. The thought of it being razed to the ground, replaced by some sterile monstrosity, left me aching. And Trent had known this all along, silently complicit in its destruction. The betrayal cut deep, sharper than I could have ever imagined.

I barreled out the leaded glass door, standing alone in the long, winding driveway with its line of Beemers, Bentleys, and Porsches.

Crap! Why were there no taxis in the Hamptons?

,I fought to yank my cellphone out of the too-small designer clutch I had paid way too much money for trying to impress. I snorted. A waste on so many levels. I tugged and tugged until the phone finally gave and I socked myself in the eye.

"Sonofabitch!" I yowled.

Yeah. That was gonna leave a mark.

But it was the least of my worries, I thought as I jabbed in a request for an Uber.

Tears burned at the inside corners of my eyes.

Oh, hell no.

I was not ruining this two-hour makeup job I'd watched countless YouTube videos learning. I willed them away even though the weight of the conversation I'd overheard pressed down on me like a storm cloud.

The mansion loomed behind me, grand and imposing, but all I could feel was the bitter sting of betrayal. Trent caught up, jogging down the steps, his polished shoes echoing across the pavement. I steeled myself, my pulse racing, the question burning my tongue.

"Is it true?" I asked, cutting through the small talk he'd opened with. "You're planning to buy out and tear down Vitello's?"

He froze, taken aback, but quickly recovered, a carefully controlled expression slipping over his face. "Annie, come on. We're getting married in less than two days. The whole family is here—"

"Answer the question, Trent." My voice came out sharper than I'd expected, my frustration and hurt slipping through every syllable. "Do you plan to demolish Vitello's?"

He hesitated, glancing around as if searching for an escape. But then he sighed, looking down at his polished shoes for a beat before meeting my gaze. "It's a smart business decision, Annie. You have to understand that."

A cold shock ran through me, and for a

second, I thought he'd been joking. But his expression was serious, his face set in that same detached way he'd worn all night. A spark of anger ignited in my chest.

"So, you're telling me that everything I poured into that place—everything Louie's built for years—it's all just a 'business decision' to you?"

"Annie, you're getting emotional," he said, his tone infuriatingly calm, as if my reaction were some unfortunate inconvenience. "It's just a building. With the right investment, you could have something even better, something that aligns with my family's vision. You'll be the head chef; you'll get all the creative freedom you need."

His words left a bitter taste in my mouth. "Just a building?" I repeated, my voice rising. "Vitello's is more than some property to be bulldozed. It's Louie's life's work. It's a part of the community! Do you even care?"

He looked at me, almost pitying. "Annie, this is how progress works. It's business. I thought you'd understand that by now."

I swallowed, his words twisting like a knife. "So, I'm supposed to watch you tear down everything that's mattered to me? And somehow, I'm just supposed to stand there and smile, as long as I get my name on a shiny new building?"

"I mean, technically, it's my name," he

mused. I glowered at him and stalked off.

"But it will be yours soon!" He chased after me. "Come on, Annie…"

He reached for my arm, but I pulled back, a resolve settling in my gut. "I thought we were partners, Trent. I thought you cared about what I wanted, what I believed in. But I'm just another accessory to you, aren't I? Just like Vitello's — a convenient piece in your family's grand plan."

He opened his mouth to argue, but I didn't wait to hear it. I turned away, feeling the weight of everything crumble as the Uber app showed Raoul would pull up at the gate shortly in a white Tesla, license plate 5EX 2407. I laughed.

Even the damned Uber drivers had it better in the Hamptons!

"Annie, you're overreacting," Trent said, his voice taking on that frustratingly calm tone, like he was trying to pacify a child. "It's just business. One day, you'll look back and understand. It's nothing personal — it's the way things work in the real world."

"Real world?" I stared at him, stunned, trying to process what I was hearing. Did he really think I was being naïve, that my passion for Vitello's and everything it stood for was just some childish attachment? "Real world? Trent Parker, you wouldn't know the 'real world' if it scrolled across the NASDAQ ticker."

"Look," he said, straightening his collar as if this was just another boardroom negotiation, "I get that you're emotional about this place. You spent years working there, and it's natural to feel connected, but that doesn't mean you can't move on to something better. You deserve more than some rundown restaurant in the middle of the city. You could have a brand-new restaurant, state-of-the-art, right there with my family's support. You'd be at the forefront of something big. Imagine the possibilities."

I felt my hands clench, the anger building. "You think this is just about a restaurant?" I asked, my voice shaking. "Vitello's is part of who I am. It's where I became a chef, where I found family and a place in the world."

He looked at me, his expression unwavering, like he was politely tolerating some amusing sentimentality. "You're clinging to the past, Annie. If you'd just let go and see the potential here, you'd understand. This is what people do when they're serious about their careers. We make hard choices, we let go of things that don't fit the future."

His words hit hard, and a deep sadness seeped in, mingling with my anger. It wasn't just the restaurant he didn't understand—it was everything. My dreams, my values, my drive, all dismissed as "clinging to the past." I felt the pieces of the life we'd planned slipping through my fingers, as if they'd never been real to him.

As Trent kept talking, his words blurred into one long string of corporate-speak: "vision," "legacy," "opportunity." I could practically see the shiny brochure he had in his head — the one where I'd play the role of the quiet, supportive wife with big hair and an empty smile, attending luncheons, nodding politely, and ignoring any hint of an actual opinion.

When I wasn't toiling in his father's restaurant making money, that is.

But with every polished, soulless word that fell from his lips, something shifted inside me. I wasn't part of his "vision." I was a footnote, a convenient prop in a life planned down to the last empty, glittering detail.

A surge of clarity struck, and with it, a sense of strength that left me almost giddy. Here I was, standing in the middle of a driveway larger than my entire apartment building, realizing that the man I'd thought I could spend my life with didn't have a clue who I really was.

I glanced at him, still rambling on as if a presentation slide had gotten stuck, and felt a spark of defiance rising. Vitello's wasn't just a "quaint old restaurant" to be bulldozed and forgotten — it was a piece of me, of my journey. And he didn't get that. Maybe he never would.

"Trent," I interrupted, cutting through his spiel mid-sentence. He blinked, startled, as if he hadn't noticed I was still here.

"I think I finally understand something," I said, a confidence I hadn't felt in a long time washing over me. "I'm not meant to be a silent partner in a polished brochure. I'm not the person who stands by while you 'build a legacy' by tearing down everything I care about."

I straightened, the weight of the last few minutes falling away as I looked him in the eye. "I'm not here to fit into anyone's world but my own. And right now, I'm realizing that's the only one I want to build."

I took a steadying breath, letting it fill my lungs, grounding me. This was it, the line I'd thought I could ignore, but it was right there, as undeniable as ever. I looked at Trent, his expression finally showing a flicker of something real—maybe surprise, maybe disbelief—but it was too little, too late.

"Trent," I began, my voice wavering only slightly, "I can't go through with this. With us." The words hung in the air, but they felt right. "You don't respect what matters to me, and I can't just overlook that."

He blinked, confusion flickering across his face as if I were speaking in riddles. "Annie, you're blowing this out of proportion. We're talking about a business decision. Vitello's is —"

"Vitello's isn't just a business decision," I interrupted, my voice firming as I found my footing. "It's a place that gave me purpose and a community. It's a part of me. And if you can't see that, then you don't see me, Trent."

He scoffed, hands on his hips. "You're throwing away our future over some run-down restaurant?"

I shook my head, feeling a surge of determination. "No, Trent. I'm choosing *my* future — the one where I don't have to cut out parts of myself to fit into someone else's expectations."

The look of disbelief on his face only fueled my resolve. "I will not marry someone who treats my dreams like they're disposable. I've worked too hard to be the person I am today, and I won't give that up to be a convenient accessory in your life."

For a moment, the silence stretched, and I could see him struggling to grasp what I was saying, as if the concept was entirely foreign to him. Maybe it was. I was finally putting myself first, standing up for the things that truly mattered to me, and the weight lifting off my shoulders was staggering.

He opened his mouth to argue, but I held up a hand, stopping him. "It's over, Trent. I deserve someone who doesn't just want me to fit into their world, but who wants to build one with me." With one last look, I turned away, feeling a powerful mix of sadness, pride, and fierce freedom.

Trent stared at me as if I'd just declared I was joining the circus. For a moment, his mouth opened and closed, and he looked almost... stunned. But he quickly recovered, straightening his posture, trying to keep his polished composure.

"Annie, you're being... emotional," he said, with a careful, patronizing tone that only made my stomach churn. "This is just a... a pet project. You can't honestly be willing to throw away everything we've built for the sake of some hole-in-the-wall restaurant. You're not seeing the big picture here."

"Vitello's is *not* just a pet project," I shot back, holding his gaze. "And I'd never 'throw away' anything that mattered."

He softened his voice like he was trying to talk me off a ledge. "Annie, think about it. Stability, a respected name, resources — these are the things that make a future worth having. I can offer you all of that. We can make a life together, one that doesn't involve scraping by in a cramped kitchen."

"Scraping by in a cramped kitchen made

me the chef I am," I replied, feeling the fire reignite in my chest. "No. It's what made *me* who I am. And if you can't see how much that means to me, then you don't understand me at all."

His jaw clenched, his frustration finally cracking through his composed exterior. "I'm trying to give you something better, Annie. I'm offering you a life most people would dream of."

But that was just it, wasn't it? He was offering me *his* dream. And for the first time, I felt absolutely certain it wasn't mine.

"Maybe it's a dream for you, Trent," I said, my voice steady, "but it's not one I want."

I could see the realization beginning to dawn in his eyes, the shock slowly giving way to something harder, and I knew, right then, that this was the end.

The app dinged. *Your Uber has arrived. Meet at pickup point.*

"Goodbye, Trent." I managed a small, resolute smile, catching his shocked expression one last time before I turned on my heel.

Walking down the sprawling driveway of his parents' estate, I felt a strange mix of emotions swirling inside me. There was sadness, sure, but there was also a surge of freedom that pushed it back. With every step, the weight of expectations, rules, and limitations peeled away, leaving only... me.

The whole place seemed to glisten in its over-polished splendor, the grand arches and marble walkways gleaming in the light, but it all felt hollow. This world, as glamorous as it was, wasn't mine—and I finally knew it with every fiber of my being.

As I neared the gate and, apparently, Raoul, I took a deep breath, feeling the cool night air fill my lungs, clear and liberating. The future ahead was uncertain, but it was *mine* now. A slow, genuine smile spread across my face. I couldn't remember the last time I'd felt so at home in my own skin.

The security guard raised an eyebrow as I reached the gate, giving me a sympathetic smile. "Leaving the party early?" he asked, opening it for me.

I let out a small laugh. "Oh, trust me. I stayed *way* too long."

Chapter Twenty-Two

Trent

I pulled out my phone as I stepped onto the sidewalk, my thumb hovering over Annie's name. For the third time that morning, I hit "CALL".

One ring. Two.

Voicemail.

"You've reached Annie McGowan. I'm probably covered in flour or yelling at an oven. Leave a message!"

I clenched my jaw, resisting the urge to hurl my phone into the nearest trash can.

Damn it, Annie. Pick up.

The cab idled at the curb, waiting for me to climb in. But I couldn't. Not yet. I needed to hear her voice — needed to say something, anything that would fix the damage between us.

I tried again. Straight to voicemail.

She wasn't just ignoring me. *She was done with me.*

The thought sent a sharp ache through my ribs, but I shoved it down and forced my legs to move. This wasn't over. Not yet.

I turned on my heel and strode toward the glass doors of Parker Enterprises.

The towering glass façade of Parker Enterprises loomed over me as I stepped out of the black sedan and onto the sleek pavement. The building was a monument to everything my father had built — precision, power, control.

The revolving doors spun with silent efficiency as I entered the lobby, the hush of polished floors and muted conversations instantly pressing against me. The scent of rich leather, expensive cologne, and freshly brewed coffee filled the air — the smell of deals being made.

I exhaled sharply, adjusting my cufflinks as I strode toward the elevator bank. I wasn't supposed to be here. Not today.

I was supposed to be fixing my relationship.

Instead, I'd gotten a clipped message from my father's assistant this morning:

Charles Parker requests your presence at headquarters. Immediately.

No explanation. No details. Just a summons.

It had been a long time since my father had *requested* anything from me.

The cold elevator walls mirrored my expression back at me — neutral, unreadable. It was a skill I'd perfected over the years. A necessity when dealing with Charles Parker.

I knew better than to expect a warm father-son chat.

As I strode past the front desk, the receptionist — an older woman with not a single hair out of place — stiffened slightly, her manicured fingers pausing over her keyboard.

"Your father is expecting you," she said.

I nodded once, but my gut tightened. There was something different in her tone.

This wasn't just about business.

I adjusted my cuffs, squared my shoulders. Whatever was waiting for me upstairs, it wasn't good.

Charles Parker didn't look up as I entered.

He was flipping through a stack of neatly arranged papers, his movements unhurried, deliberate. As if I wasn't even there. As if this was just another meeting.

No greeting. No pleasantries. Just a flick of his wrist, an unspoken order to sit.

I clenched my jaw, lowering myself into the leather chair across from him. I hated how transactional this always felt, how every interaction was a negotiation rather than a conversation.

The silence stretched, thick as molasses.

Then, without looking up, he spoke. Calm. Measured.

"I'm judging a competition."

I frowned.

Not what I expected.

I thought he called me in for a postmortem on my disaster of a relationship. A lecture. Maybe an offer to clean up my mess.

But I should've known better. Charles Parker didn't waste time mourning failures. He only worked to control them.

"A competition?"

Finally, he lifted his gaze, pinning me with that sharp, unreadable stare.

"Whisk It All. Final round."

The words hit like a gut punch.

My fingers curled around the armrest, tension creeping into my spine.

I stared at him, waiting for the punchline.

He scratched out a signature and shuffled some papers. "It was a last-minute decision."

Charles Parker did not do last-minute decisions. Every move he made was calculated weeks — months — in advance. There was always a strategy, a carefully mapped-out endgame. He didn't waste time on frivolous things like culinary competitions.

I narrowed my eyes. "You don't even believe in competitions."

He finally leaned back in his chair, his expression unreadable but his posture entirely at ease. That was the thing about my father — he never had to raise his voice to make himself heard. Power, when wielded properly, never needed volume.

He flicked a hand through the air, as if swatting away my concern like an annoying gnat. "Competitions are useful when you know how to leverage them."

My stomach twisted.

This wasn't about prestige or networking. He was positioning himself.

To control the outcome. To control Annie. *To control... me.*

Heat prickled at the base of my neck. "Why this one?" My voice was steady, but my fingers curled into fists against my thighs.

He didn't answer immediately. Just studied me with the same detached calculation he reserved for business deals.

A quiet confirmation that I was just another variable in his equation.

He smoothed the cuff of his pristine, custom-tailored suit—a deliberate pause, just long enough to let me feel the weight of his silence. Then, with the ease of a man who had never once lacked information, he smirked. "How do you think I always scoop up the hottest chefs?" His tone was almost amused. "Someone's got to keep their finger on the pulse."

A slow, sick realization settled in my gut.

He'd known. Before the press, before the public, before me.

Because of course he had.

Charles Parker wasn't a judge by coincidence. He had contacts inside the competition board — people who owed him favors, people who whispered things in exchange for future opportunities. A name like his didn't just open doors; it built them.

"You knew," I murmured, the words tasting bitter.

His smirk widened slightly. "I make it a point to know things before the rest of the world does. That's how you stay ahead, son."

The room tilted — not physically, but in the way that happens when a truth knocks the air out of you.

This wasn't about Parker Enterprises. It wasn't about market expansion, business leverage, or brand prestige.

Charles Parker wasn't just orchestrating a strategic play.

He was proving he was better than me.

The realization hit like a punch to the ribs. He'd always considered me a variable, a moving piece on his board — but this? This was different. This was personal.

He hadn't trusted me to handle things. He hadn't believed in me for a red-hot second.

My jaw tightened. *"Jesus Christ."* I exhaled sharply, gripping the arms of the chair. "You *never* trusted me to manage this, did you?"

Charles didn't flinch.

Didn't blink.

Didn't even pretend to soften the blow.

He merely adjusted his cufflinks and said, "Was I wrong?"

There it was. The truth stripped bare. His father had never thought he was capable — not of handling the business, not of controlling the outcome, not of keeping Annie. Trent had spent years proving himself in boardrooms and strategy meetings, but it had never been about skill. It had always been about trust. And Charles Parker had never trusted him. Not really.

Something inside me fractured.

Not a crack — a break. A clean, sharp split between who I'd been raised to be and the man I was choosing to become.

I had spent my life playing Parker games. Mastering the rules, staying inside the lines, nodding along while my father moved pieces around a board only he could see. I had made peace with it — or so I thought.

But this?

This wasn't business.

This was Annie.

And Charles Parker would not decide her

future.

Heat rushed through my veins, but my voice was smooth when I stood, pushing back my chair. "Well. Good luck with that, Dad."

A flicker of something — surprise, maybe — crossed his face. It was gone in an instant.

"Where are you going?"

I met his gaze without hesitation.

"To make sure you don't get away with it."

For the first time in my life, I walked away from a Parker deal before it could be sealed.

And for the first time in my life, I didn't give a damn about the consequences.

*****

I stepped out of my father's office and into the hallway, but the air still felt thick with him. Like the walls had absorbed his control, his expectations, his damn certainty that everything would go exactly as he intended.

My pulse hammered in my ears as I took long, deliberate strides toward the elevator, but my thoughts were anything but controlled. They were chaos.

I hit the down button harder than necessary, willing the doors to open faster.

Charles Parker had spent his entire life manipulating outcomes. But this time? This time, he had gone too far. He wasn't just stacking the deck—he was dealing the cards himself.

And Annie had no idea.

A muscle clenched in my jaw as the elevator doors slid open. I stepped inside, the cold metal reflecting my own unreadable expression back at me.

For years, I had let him dictate everything. Where I worked, who I did business with, who I became.

But not this. *Not her.*

As the elevator descended, one thought cut through the storm raging in my head.

I needed to get to Annie. And I needed to get to her fast.

The moment I stepped out of the Parker Enterprises building, I yanked my phone from my pocket and dialed Annie.

Still nothing but voicemail.

"You've reached Annie McGowan. I'm probably covered in flour or yelling at an oven. Leave a message!"

Damn it.

I swore under my breath and tried again, pacing along the sidewalk, dodging pedestrians who threw me annoyed glances as I muttered curses into the cold air.

My grip tightened around the phone. She was probably at the competition. Of course she was. And I'd wasted time playing my father's game when I should have been fighting for her.

I exhaled sharply, forcing myself to think.

This wasn't just about warning Annie. It was about making sure Charles couldn't rig her future like he had every other damn thing in my life.

I didn't know exactly how he planned to do it, but I knew one thing for certain.

If my father was on that judging panel, Annie didn't stand a chance.

And I refused to let that happen.

I shoved my phone back into my pocket, jaw clenched so tight my teeth ached.

What the hell was I doing?

There was no plan. No strategy. No carefully calculated move to outmaneuver my father. I had spent my entire life playing by his rules, anticipating his next play, ensuring I never made a misstep that would land me outside the Parker empire's carefully controlled boundaries.

And yet, here I was, about to bulldoze straight through the walls he had built.

For Annie.

A sharp breath left me, my pulse hammering in my ears. Why did it take this to wake me up? I'd been coasting, pretending my life was exactly what I wanted—pretending I could shape it into something that fit me if I just tried hard enough. But the truth was glaring now, impossible to ignore.

Maybe I wasn't made for this world as much as I had believed.

Not my father's version of it, anyway.

Annie had always seen something in me — something real, something better. Something worth saving.

And maybe, for the first time in my life, I believed her.

I wasn't just fighting my father anymore.

I was fighting for myself.

I stepped off the curb, arm raised, signaling for a cab. The moment the yellow car jerked to a stop, I yanked the door open and slid inside, heart hammering like a war drum.

"Where to?" the driver asked, glancing at me through the rearview mirror.

"Brooklyn Expo Center. Now." My voice was steel. No hesitation. No second-guessing.

The driver pulled into traffic, weaving through the congested streets. I barely noticed. My mind was already there, inside the competition, moving past security, past the cameras, past the perfectly polished judges' table where my father would sit — a king pretending to be impartial while deciding Annie's fate.

Not today.

If Charles Parker thought he could rig the

game, I was about to break the damn board.

For years, I had played by his rules, accepting the fact that my life — my choices — were never truly my own. But Annie wasn't his to control.

She belonged in that kitchen. Not as some stepping stone in his corporate portfolio. Not as a casualty of his ambition.

I clenched my fists.

I didn't care what it cost me.

I was going to that competition.

And I wasn't leaving until I leveled the playing field

Chapter Twenty-Three

Annie

I stepped into the competition venue, and it felt like a tiny marching band was parading in my stomach. The thrill of competing was there, but it was buried under the avalanche of everything riding on this one day.

And maybe, if I were being honest, it wasn't just the competition knotting my stomach. It was everything else. The breakup. The mess I'd left in my wake. The fact that I could still hear Trent's voice in my head, echoing words I didn't want to think about. This wasn't just a shot at redemption for Vitello's.

I told myself I was fine. That the break-up was the right move. That I didn't need Trent's apologies or explanations. But standing here, heart pounding, I realized something unsettling—he had believed in me. Maybe in a twisted, Parker, business-first kind of way, but he had believed in me. And now, if I failed today, I wouldn't just be proving his father right. I'd be proving Trent wrong, too.

Adjusting the lanyard around my neck, I took in the other contestants, each of them looking cool, calm, and collected. I envied them. They didn't have a restaurant to save, a career to rebuild, or a wedding to hold. This wasn't just a culinary showdown; it was my high-stakes rom-com climax, complete with a handsome antagonist lurking somewhere around here.

My mind darted through every choice that had led me to this point—the late nights, the risky moves, Louie's words about Vitello's closing day echoing in my head. I'd sworn to myself this wouldn't end in a heartbreakingly empty dining room. This was about keeping Vitello's alive, and, if all went well, a little sweet revenge, too.

Because what else did I have left? A hollow apartment and a voicemail from Louie telling me to "focus on what matters." Well, this was what mattered. This was the only thing that still felt like mine.

I squared my shoulders, inhaled the aroma of garlic and basil in the air and let the energy of the place ground me. Today, I'd give it everything—because Vitello's and I both deserved this win.

Across the room, I caught sight of Jordan, and wouldn't you know it, he was looking like a cover model for *Chef Monthly*—all focused, intense, and, annoyingly, still way too attractive. I could practically feel the smug determination radiating off him, like he was here not just to cook but to settle some grand score. Part of me wanted to roll my eyes. The other part wanted to march over and remind him he wasn't the only one with something to prove.

I forced myself to take a breath, grounding myself. This was my shot, too—my chance to keep Vitello's going, and maybe even show Jordan that he wasn't the only one with a few new tricks up his sleeve. If he thought he'd be sailing through this competition, well, he had another think coming. In fact, it was almost invigorating. If this was going to turn into a showdown, then bring it on.

A local news crew bustled in, cameras and microphones at the ready, adding a sudden flare of drama to the room.

Great—no pressure at all.

I adjusted my apron, hyper-aware of how many eyes were on me. I wasn't just fighting for a title—I was fighting for my future. I was fighting for proof that I was more than a failed engagement, a business on the brink, and a woman stupid enough to believe she could have it all.

As the reporters tested their mics and the cameraman zoomed in on the kitchen stations, I closed my eyes, murmured a few fumbling affirmations and tried to manifest the headlines: *Small-Town Chef Shines!* or *Local Girl's Cooking Steals the Show!* The key, of course, was making it look easy — effortless, even — while not accidentally tossing flour all over myself. After all, I was here to impress the judges *and* anyone watching, and if it took a little kitchen theater, then hey, let the games begin.

The competition floor was humming with tension, but the energy only intensified as the news crew prepared for their contestant introductions. Microphone in hand, a reporter began gliding through the stations, giving each chef their spotlight, while the cameraman zoomed in with a cinematic sweep.

First up was Chef Rico. Tall, polished, and radiating an air of effortless sophistication, he looked like he belonged on the cover of *Gourmet Weekly*. His pristine white chef's coat gleamed under the lights, accented by a subtle fleur-de-lis pin at the collar.

With a smooth French accent, he declared, "Ah, zis eez not competition — it eez art. I am here to inspire and elevate." As he deftly sliced into a truffle, the spectators sighed in unison, clearly under his spell.

Next, the camera panned to Chef Tanya. Barely five feet tall but commanding the room with her energy, she stirred her pot with the intensity of a Formula 1 driver. Her apron was a patchwork of competition badges, and her biceps flexed as she flipped her spatula with flair. "I didn't come to play, sweetheart," she said in a thick New Jersey accent, her tone daring anyone to challenge her. "Back home, soggy pasta gets you booed out of the kitchen. So, buckle up, folks."

Then the crew moved to the most talked-about chef in the room, who had ignored the competition dress code: Jordan. A smirk tugged at his lips as the camera closed in, his black T-shirt accentuating biceps that had earned a few admiring glances, intentional or not. Jordan rolled a lemon between his palms, glancing at the reporter with an easy confidence.

"And you, Chef Jordan?" the reporter prompted. "What's your strategy going into today?"

"Strategy?" He flashed an easy grin, catching the lemon in one hand. "I just plan to cook my heart out and let the flavors speak for themselves." His gaze drifted in my direction for the briefest moment, adding, "I'm here to enjoy every minute. What's the fun in cooking if you're not having a good time?"

A ripple of laughter moved through the audience, but I could feel the unspoken challenge in his words. Jordan was as much here for the thrill of competition as he was to prove something—if only to himself.

At least, that was what I was telling myself.

Finally, the camera swung to me. I inhaled sharply, half-wishing the camera would veer off and half-ready to prove my worth. The reporter turned, that microphone now squarely in front of me.

"And Chef Annie," she started. "You're here representing Vitello's, the neighborhood favorite, correct?"

"That's right," I replied, managing a smile that I hoped looked more confident than I felt. I could already imagine a hundred neighbors watching from their living rooms, rooting for me and Vitello's, expecting me to make them proud.

"What makes Vitello's special?" the reporter asked, curiosity sparking in her eyes. I glanced around, feeling the weight of everyone's gaze.

"Vitello's is more than just a restaurant," I said, my voice steady but filled with emotion. "It's family, it's history, it's home. Every dish has a story, and I'm here to show that even the simplest ingredients can make magic."

The cameraman gave a thumbs up, the red light blinking off, and with that, the reporter moved on, leaving me alone with my thoughts.

The camera crew turned again to Jordan,

and I couldn't help but watch as he shifted his weight, planting his good foot with that signature confidence. Even with the cast awkwardly propped beside him, he looked completely unfazed — like he'd chosen the cast as a fashion statement to boost his rugged appeal. Typical Jordan. He flashed a grin just shy of cocky, the kind that used to make people — okay, fine, me — swoon.

But there was something else in his eyes, a glimmer of determination I hadn't expected. For all his relaxed charm, he was here to win. And that strange knot in my stomach? It twisted a little tighter.

Was he feeling as conflicted as I was?

Then he caught my eye, just for a split second, and it felt like an electric charge zapped through the air. I bit back a smirk, wondering if he realized just how much our messy history had turned up the heat in this kitchen.

Great. I had to win over the judges and *resist the urge to throw a spoon at him.*

The room quieted as a familiar voice echoed over the speakers. At the front of the room stood none other than television's culinary darling, Celeste Moretti, microphone in hand and charisma dialed up to eleven. With her dazzling trademark smile and a look that was part fire, part finesse, she swept her gaze over us, instantly commanding the room's attention.

"Chefs!" she called out, her voice effortlessly filling the room. "Welcome to the Whisk It All Ultimate Culinary Showdown!" A ripple of excitement rolled through the crowd, a mix of thrill and nerves sparking in each contestant's eyes. I felt my heart jump, reminding me of what was at stake here—not just Vitello's, but maybe a chance to reclaim a piece of myself.

Celeste continued, "Today, we'll see who's got the passion, precision, and sheer guts to take home the title. You'll each have an hour for this first round—your signature dish. Show us what you're made of!" She flashed a grin that could outshine the cameras and clapped her hands together. "Now, let's get cooking!"

And just like that, the air practically sizzled with energy as each chef dove for their stations. I couldn't help but size up my fellow contestants as I surveyed the flurry of activity around me. Everyone was setting up their own culinary mystery, and the aromas—garlic, citrus, and something smoky—were already starting to layer together like an edible symphony. I'd be lying if I said I wasn't curious.

To my right was Chef Rico, looking as polished as his truffle-infused olive oil. He was methodically lining up ingredients that screamed "refined": a small jar of saffron, white wine, and what looked suspiciously like imported chanterelles. Probably preparing something like a saffron risotto with wild mushrooms—a classic, but with his flair. He worked with careful precision, every movement smooth and deliberate, as if he were orchestrating a symphony instead of chopping an onion.

Down the line, Chef Tanya was a whirl of energy, barely pausing for breath as she prepped. Her station was a contrast to Rico's elegance, with big, bold ingredients laid out in abundance: tomatoes so red they looked like they'd been handpicked for a commercial, fistfuls of fresh basil, and a chunky wheel of Pecorino Romano that she handled like it was a weapon. She was probably whipping up something punchy, maybe an Amatriciana pasta with a heavy dose of kick. Tanya was nothing if not fearless, and that blend of ingredients promised a dish with as much personality as she had.

There were the others, chefs from around the world and close by, greeted one by one. Then, on my left, there was Jordan, his setup both suspiciously simple and incredibly tantalizing. He had laid out fresh thyme, garlic, lemon, and something wrapped in butcher paper I couldn't quite make out.

My stomach flipped as I watched him, wondering if he was going for something subtle to show off his finesse—like lemon-thyme roasted chicken. Or maybe he'd throw in a last-minute twist. Jordan had always loved surprises, both in the kitchen and out, and his intense focus made it clear he wasn't here only to participate.

I tore my gaze away, reminding myself this wasn't just about admiring everyone's setup. This was a competition, and I was here to win.

I just had to focus. Focus on the food, on the challenge. Not on the ache that twisted in my gut when I thought about Trent and how fast everything had crumbled between us. Not on the fact that, as much as I tried to push him from my mind, part of me still wondered if he was watching, if he was thinking about me too.

My station was stocked with everything I needed for my puttanesca-inspired seared scallops—a little briny, a little bold, and full of flavor. Taking a deep breath, I felt a surge of excitement. The room crackled with anticipation, each of us silently daring the others to bring their best.

I wasn't just cooking for a title, though—I was cooking to prove something. To prove to Louie that I hadn't let him down. To prove to myself that I was more than a woman Trent Parker betrayed. And maybe, in some buried, shameful part of me, to prove to Trent that I was still worth betting on.

As I seared the scallops in my pan, I could feel Jordan's eyes on me, flickering over like a spark catching fire. He was standing a few stations down, chopping herbs with a fury that suggested he was imagining the parsley was someone's head—mine, probably. But even with the tension practically sizzling between us, there was this…oddly charged, almost magnetic pull.

I tried to focus on my sauce, stirring in olives and capers, but every time I dared glance up, I'd catch him scowling over his chopping board, his expression a mix of irritation and something else I couldn't quite name. It was so intense I half-expected him to stalk over and demand I hand over his lemon zester or something.

For a moment, I was back in Granny's old kitchen, teasing him into sharing his tricks, leaning too close to peek at his—ahem—sauce. Now, though, it was a different game entirely, and instead of playful sparks, we were dealing with a full-on culinary standoff with an egg timer counting down to high noon.

A horrified "Mon Dieu!" erupted from Rico's station, snapping everyone's attention his way. He stood frozen, glaring at his chopping board as if it had betrayed him.

"This… this is cilantro!" he sputtered, poking at the leafy green pile with exaggerated disgust. "I asked for parsley! Curly leaf parsley!"

Across the room, Tanya raised an eyebrow, barely hiding her smirk. "Really, Rico? They look nothing alike."

Rico's jaw dropped. "I have created a masterpiece of Mediterranean elegance, and this — this imposter has ruined it!" He flung the offending herb aside with a dramatic flourish. "Who puts cilantro next to parsley, anyway?"

As Rico frantically fished out the remaining leaves, muttering about "herbaceous sabotage," Jordan and I caught each other's eyes, stifling grins. The tension in the room briefly eased, replaced by a shared moment of absurdity.

As I stirred my sauce, I couldn't help but notice Jordan a few stations down, radiating that infuriating calm, like he was hosting a cooking show rather than competing. Every time I sneaked a look, there he was — focused, steady, and, of course, looking my way too. It was as if we were both trying to out-casual each other, pretending the other wasn't there when it was painfully obvious we both were.

His chopping was almost annoyingly precise, each slice of the knife landing with a satisfying *thunk* that seemed to say, *Yep, still watching you.* In retaliation, I gave my sauce a dramatic stir, like I was demonstrating the perfect wrist technique, hoping he'd see I wasn't about to let him throw me off. But every time I did, he'd arch an eyebrow, a hint of a smirk on his face.

Our dishes were becoming some bizarre silent code, and every dash of salt or slice of lemon felt like a mini showdown. The real heat wasn't coming from the stoves—it was simmering between us, bubbling up in every competitive glance and accidental smile.

As I sautéed the garlic, the aroma rose from the pan. I realized I was pouring a lot more than olive oil into this dish. Every sprinkle of salt, every precise chop of the tomatoes, felt like I was unloading my emotions right into the pot.

Sure, there was a bit of fire in me to outdo Jordan, but that was barely scratching the surface. It went deeper, to the heart of why I'd signed up for this. Vitello's was on the line, and so was my sense of purpose. As I added fresh basil, I thought of Louie, the old recipes, the neighborhood regulars who knew every dish on the menu. It was all woven into my cooking, my own strange recipe of frustration, loyalty, and determination.

I took a deep breath, feeling the weight of it all, but also feeling stronger. This dish had to be perfect. It was as much a symbol of my future as it was a meal.

The clock ticked down, each second pounding in my ears like a drumbeat. The kitchen was a blur of flurried movement, chefs rushing to add the final touches, and I could feel the pressure boiling over. My sauce was thickening just right, the scallops perfectly seared—but then I noticed. The capers. I had no capers!

Which meant my little caper ... was about to be all for nothing.

Chapter Twenty-Four

Annie

My heart leaped into my throat. How could I forget the capers? They were crucial to the puttanesca — the briny kick that made the dish sing. I fumbled through my station, muttering in a half-panicked frenzy. "Come on, where are you? Capers, capers… capers!" My pulse pounded in my ears, drowning out the clamor of the kitchen.

Tanya snorted from a few stations away. "Amateur move, sweetheart," she quipped, her smirk loud enough to cut through the tension. My cheeks burned as the cameras zoomed in, capturing my panic for everyone to see.

Then, out of nowhere, a hand appeared in my line of vision, a small jar of capers resting in the palm. I froze, startled, as the hand gave the tiniest nudge forward.

"Can't have puttanesca without these," Jordan murmured, his voice low and calm, as though he wasn't walking straight into my whirlwind of panic. Our eyes met for a fraction of a second—just long enough for me to catch something unspoken in his gaze before he turned and strode back to his station. The jar of capers sat cool in my palm, an anchor in the middle of the chaos.

For a moment, I couldn't move. The gesture—so unexpected, so perfectly timed—sent a ripple through me I couldn't quite name.

Was it gratitude? Annoyance? Some messy cocktail of both?

My fingers tightened around the jar as my thoughts whirled. Was this pity? Was he trying to throw me off my game? Or…was this just Jordan being Jordan, the guy who used to make me laugh in the middle of our most heated kitchen disasters?

I stared at the jar in my hand, the weight of it suddenly feeling heavier than it should. I glanced at him, but his attention was already back on his own dish, slicing through herbs with infuriating ease. The past was simmering just below the surface, bubbling up in ways I hadn't prepared for.

"Focus," I whispered to myself, shaking off the static in my head. The sauce bubbled angrily in the pan, demanding my attention.

I threw a handful of capers into the mix, stirring furiously to catch up. The briny aroma hit my nose almost immediately, and something clicked—like the dish itself was relieved to be complete. The panic ebbed as the sauce thickened, each movement of the spoon grounding me a little more.

But the jar of capers still sat on my station, a quiet reminder of Jordan's presence. As I plated my scallops, I caught myself glancing in his direction. He was focused on his dish, his knife moving with the same precision I'd admired—maybe envied—back when we'd worked side by side. For all his smugness, there was something genuine about him in moments like these. It was infuriating.

Still, as the clock ticked down, I couldn't shake the feeling that those capers weren't just an ingredient. They were a message—one I wasn't quite ready to decode.

From somewhere overhead, the commentator's voice crackled. "In an unexpected twist, Chef Jordan has just assisted his rival, Chef Annie, by providing her with capers! You don't see that every day, folks!"

I stood there, stunned, the jar of capers staring at me. But I didn't have time to dwell on it. I spooned the sauce over the scallops with every bit of focus I had, feeling a strange warmth where he'd touched my hand.

The clock hit zero, and the room buzzed as chefs stepped back from their stations, panting and wiping their brows. We were all on edge, watching the judges inspect each dish with meticulous care. The air practically crackled with anticipation, but as they approached Chef Rico's station, I noticed his expression—confident, bordering on smug. He stood tall, hands behind his back, waiting for the praise he clearly expected.

The head judge took a bite of his saffron risotto, his face unreadable. Rico's jaw tensed, eyes narrowing as the judge paused, glanced at his fellow judges, and exchanged a brief nod. Then, with a raised eyebrow, the judge turned to Rico. "Chef Rico, I'm sorry, but your dish has not made the cut. Thank you for participating."

A collective gasp rippled through the kitchen. Rico's eyes widened, his face an explosion of indignation. "You're cutting *me*? Do you even know what saffron is? Do you know how difficult it is to achieve this level of refinement?" He gestured wildly at his risotto, which now seemed to radiate with the disappointment of his culinary dreams.

The judges remained calm, but Rico's voice climbed higher with each word. "This competition is clearly biased! My dish is a masterpiece, a symphony of flavors!"

"Yeah," Chef Tanya snickered. "Saffron and soap. That's whatcha get with cilantro, baby."

"And you!" He pointed at the her. "You wouldn't know fine cuisine if it danced on your palate!"

I caught Jordan's eye from across the room, and we both fought back smiles. It was a relief, a shared moment of humor in this tense battlefield. Rico continued his tirade, his hands slicing the air as if conducting his own indignant orchestra, until the judges finally guided him out.

The competition was fierce, but for that split second, the pressure eased as Jordan and I shared a look that said, *Can you believe this guy?*

The judge stepped forward, clipboard in hand, and the room fell silent, every chef holding their breath. My heart pounded, thundering in my chest as I waited. It all came down to this moment—had I done enough? Had the capers saved me?

One by one, names were announced. The first few, I barely registered, every fiber of my being focused on hearing one word: *Annie.* I gripped the edge of my station, pretending calm, but inside I was a bundle of nerves and wild hope. My mind raced with everything this competition meant—Vitello's, my career, the risks I'd taken to get here.

"Chef Annie," the judge called, his voice cutting through the silence.

I exhaled, a flood of relief and pride surging

through me. I'd made it to the next round. Somehow, the capers, the late-night practices, the stress — it had all been worth it, at least for now. I could feel my lips pulling into a smile, and as I glanced across the room, my gaze caught Jordan's. For just a moment, I let myself feel it: the pride, the excitement, the sense that, maybe, I could actually pull this off.

"Chef Jordan."

The judge's voice rang out, and I felt an odd swirl of emotions I hadn't expected. Relief, oddly enough, was the first — a sense of quiet satisfaction that he'd made it, that he wouldn't walk away now with that look of betrayal still etched on his face. But right on its heels came another realization: my toughest competition was staying right here in the game.

I glanced over to see his reaction. Jordan's face, usually so composed, softened into a quick smile, and he gave a small nod, that flicker of pride unmistakable. The sight made my chest tighten, both with the memory of how good he was and the reminder of exactly who I was up against. We'd both fought hard to get here, and now, in this strange way, it felt like a game of chess. Each move mattered, and each small victory only tightened the stakes between us.

He looked up, and for a second, our eyes met, his gaze filled with that fierce determination I knew too well. I forced myself to turn back to my station, grounding myself. If I wanted to win this, I couldn't afford to lose focus—not even for him.

After the announcements, I barely had time to savor the moment before a news crew swept in with their cameras, capturing every expression, every sigh of relief, and every flash of disappointment. I tried to look calm, professional, but when I glanced up, there it was—a monitor showing live footage from around the room, and right next to my face was Jordan's.

Film at eleven.

I grimaced.

Our expressions side by side felt almost comical: me, smiling with barely contained triumph; Jordan, with that ever-present smirk, his eyes glinting with some secret challenge meant just for me.

With a grin, he leaned in just close enough that only I could hear. "Remember when we used to cook side-by-side? How…hot…the kitchen was?"

"Would you cut it out?" I squirmed in my checkered chef pants.

He leaned in closer. "This is hotter." His voice was teasing, laced with the familiarity that reminded me just how close we used to be.

He was doing this on purpose. Trying to throw me off. But I wasn't about to give him the satisfaction. Two could play this game.

"Yeah, and as I recall, one of us got...burned."

Ha! That knocked the cheeky grin off his face.

Suddenly, a voice from behind us piped up, "Did you say you two used to cook together?" One reporter had caught wind of the conversation, and suddenly, her eyes sparkled with a gleam I recognized all too well — the thrill of a juicy story.

"Oh, we cooked, alright," Jordan smiled that stupid, gorgeous, disarming smile.

Yeah. We cooked. My goose!

I felt my cheeks go red. This was not the attention I wanted right now.

Another reporter's eyes lit up. "So, you two were an item?"

Jordan shrugged, clearly enjoying the attention as he leaned casually on his crutches. "Guess you could say that." He shot me a quick, mischievous look that made my pulse skip. "But that was a while ago."

The first reporter stepped closer, microphone at the ready. "How does it feel, competing against each other now?"

"Well, I—" I fumbled, glancing toward the cameras, hoping my face wasn't as red as it felt. "It's a professional competition, you know? We're both just here to do our best." I tried to wave it off with a professional smile, but they weren't about to let go that easily.

"So, no hard feelings?" another reporter pressed, her gaze flitting between us, practically salivating at the hint of drama.

Jordan shot her an easy smile, all charm. "Hey, just because we're not together anymore doesn't mean I don't respect Annie's talent." He turned to me, a glimmer of something in his eye that I couldn't quite place. "She's great." He seemed to stumble. "I mean, she's a great... chef."

I held my breath. For a moment, it was like all the cameras, all the animosity... it all melted away. I pulled at my collar.

Was it getting hotter in here?

One reporter cleared their throat, reminding me where I was.

"Oh?" I shot back, arching a brow, more to keep from melting than to play along. "Then you might want to brace yourself for some *stiff* competition."

The reporters loved that, practically circling in with renewed energy. Unfortunately, so did Jordan. My unintentional double entendre fanned the flame.

Damn it! Why did my brain turned to Quaker Oats every time Jordan was around?

"Do you think your history adds some tension to the kitchen?" someone else called,

222

pushing a microphone even closer.

"Oh, there's tension, alright," Jordan murmured under his breath, just low enough for only me to hear, though he barely held back a smirk. I shot him a look that said, *not helping,* but his smile only grew.

"Care to elaborate on that tension?" a reporter piped up eagerly, and suddenly I found myself in a spotlight I definitely hadn't expected.

"Well," I said, floundering a bit, "we're both very... passionate."

Eyebrows raised. Laughs tittered.

I waved my hands frantically. "About food! We're both very passionate about *food*." The reporters chuckled, eating up every vague answer I tried to give.

"Passion in the kitchen and out, then?" another asked, not missing a beat.

Before I could respond, Jordan stepped in, all charm and composure. "We're just here to cook, folks," he said, but the twinkle in his eye told me he was enjoying this way too much. "If there's drama, I guess it'll just have to be in the dishes."

The questions kept coming, a relentless flood of interest that made my head spin. Somewhere, buried beneath all the ridiculousness, I felt a familiar thrill—it was absurd and awkward, but I'd be lying if I said it wasn't fun.

I wasn't the only one feeling a charge. The energy in the room had ticked up more than a few notches as it seemed the reporters had found their perfect narrative—a pair of former flames turned rivals, both advancing, both cooking with something to prove. I looked at the camera pushing in for an uncomfortable closeup of the two of us.

As if sensing my gaze, Jordan looked over at the monitor, his eyebrow quirking when he saw our faces together on the screen. He turned back to me, his lips curving into a grin that was practically magnetic. "Guess *we're* the show now," he murmured, just loud enough for me to hear over the buzz of the room.

I forced a nonchalant shrug. "If they're looking for drama, they're in the right place," I replied, keeping my tone light but feeling my cheeks warm as his gaze lingered.

He laughed softly, leaning in just a fraction. "Good thing you're not the only one bringing the heat, then."

I swallowed, the challenge in his voice lighting a spark somewhere between excitement and…well, maybe more excitement than I'd care to admit. This wasn't just competition anymore; it was a story, our story, written in food, in shared glances, in every accidental brush of hands over a stray ingredient.

As the cameras finally moved on, I straightened my apron and took a steadying breath. My fingers grazed the edge of my station, anchoring me in the familiar rhythm of the kitchen. The reporters, the questions, and Jordan's maddening charm — they were background noise now. What mattered was the work in front of me, the promise I made to myself, to Vitello's, and to everyone counting on me.

Across the room, I felt his gaze burn into me, daring me to look up. When I did, our eyes locked, and for a second, everything else blurred — the cameras, the crowd, the clanging pots and pans. It was just us, locked in a challenge as familiar as it was electric.

I tilted my head, letting the smallest smile tug at my lips.

Bring it on.

His smirk flickered, just enough to tell me he caught it. Without a word, I turned back to my station, knife in hand, my focus sharp as the blade. Whatever came next, I'd be ready.

This wasn't just a competition. It was war — and I had no intention of losing. Winning this wasn't just about Vitello's anymore. It was about rewriting the story — mine, not his.

For the first time in days, I felt something lift. A weight, a whisper of confidence that had been shaken loose by too many sleepless nights and second-guessing. Maybe I didn't need Trent Parker in my corner. Maybe I never had. But the nagging voice in my head asked a harder question.

Why, then, did I still want him to see this?

Chapter Twenty-Five

Annie

I'd done it. I'd really done it.

I'd made it through three rounds of elimination and was standing like a champ.

I stared at my reflection in the venue bathroom mirror, wincing at the dark smudge spreading around my left eye.

Well, maybe Rocky Balboa… after that Russian guy beat him to a pulp.

Man. I'd really done a number on myself when I'd left the engagement party that turned into a break-up party.

I looked like a freaking raccoon!

And it had all been nationally televised.

"Fantastic," I muttered.

Drawing in a deep breath, I attempted to dab fresh concealer over the bruised skin, but it wasn't doing much. If anything, I was making it worse. I paused.

Maybe if I would look fierce, like a warrior in the ultimate battle…

...or maybe I'd just look like someone who'd called off a wedding and clobbered herself.

God, I hoped not. That would just beg questions I was not prepared to answer. Finally, I just gave up.

I had barely chucked the concealer into my makeup bag when the door swung open.

I jolted, my concealer pencil slipping from my fingers as Trent stormed into the ladies' room like he owned the place.

"Oh, for the love of—" I groaned, rubbing my temples. "Trent, do you even know where you are right now?"

He wasn't listening.

His tie was slightly loosened, his hair ruffled—not Trent-like at all. And, most alarming, he looked... frantic.

"Annie, you have to listen to me." His voice was low, urgent. "I need to talk to you. It's about my father."

"Trent, whatever this is, I don't have time."

"This isn't about us."

I froze.

He was standing too close, his scent— expensive cologne and something undeniably Trent—filling the air between us.

And that look in his eyes. Desperate. Torn.

For a moment, I hesitated.

Maybe this really wasn't about us.

Then he opened his mouth again.

"Annie, I swear, I know I messed up. I should have—"

A sharp laugh escaped before I could stop it. "Nope. We're not doing this."

He pinched the bridge of his nose. "Can you let me finish a sentence?"

"Oh, I'm sorry," I said, grabbing a tissue to dab under my eyes. "I thought you came in here to confess your sins and tell me what a mistake you made—again. Like the fifty messages you left on my voicemail."

He sighed, exasperated. "I—"

The door burst open again.

A frazzled production assistant holding a clipboard practically skidded into the room, eyes wide as they landed on me, and then on...

Trent.

In the ladies' room.

"Uh..." The PA's brows shot up. "Am I interrupting something?"

I waved her off. "Nope. Just a minor case of trespassing."

"Right." The PA blinked, shifting awkwardly. "Well, you're needed on set, like, five minutes ago. The cameras are rolling, Celeste is hyped, and the producers are already stress-eating biscotti."

I nodded, hastily shoving my compact back

into my bag.

Then, without thinking, I blurted, "My fiancé was just leaving."

The words had barely left my mouth before I realized.

Trent stilled.

The PA's jaw dropped.

A beat of silence stretched before I corrected, "Ex-fiancé."

The PA exhaled dramatically. "Whew! Girl, you can't be throwing words like that around all casual."

Then she grinned, flipping through her clipboard with a teasing shake of the head. "First, Jordan Shaw, and now this guy? Damn, what are you cooking with? You gotta hook a girl up."

Trent turned to me slowly, arching an eyebrow. "Jordan Shaw?"

The PA snorted. "Oh, honey. You got competition."

Before I could respond, they clapped their hands. "All right, chop chop, superstar! You've got a competition to win."

With that, the PA spun on her heel and disappeared, leaving behind a stunned silence.

I reached for my apron, brushing past Trent without another word.

"I'm serious," he murmured, his voice softer this time. "This isn't about getting you back.

My father is rigging the competition."

I paused.

Just for a second.

Then I shook my head, shoving the thought aside. I couldn't do this. Not right now.

"You better go, Parker," I said, tightening my apron strings. "Before someone else walks in and gets the wrong idea."

And without looking back, I pushed open the door, stepping into the chaos beyond.

Because this wasn't about Trent, or his father, or whatever crisis he thought he needed to save me from.

This was my competition. My future.

And I wasn't about to let either of them mess it up.

With a last sigh, I headed into the kitchen arena. The energy of the room hit me like the aroma of fresh basil — electric, heady, and... completely nerve-wracking. My heart pounded, but not with the usual thrill of competition.

This was different. I'd walked away from a lot more than a man last night. I'd turned my back on the entire life I'd almost sold myself into, all to be here, fighting for something real.

I took a shaky breath and forced myself to focus. If I didn't give my all today, last night's sacrifice would be for nothing. Yet, despite my resolve, the fragments of last night's conversation lingered in my mind. Trent's dismissive words echoed, and a familiar, unwelcome doubt crept in.

Could I really do this?

"Well, Annie, we're about to find out," I murmured out loud. I took my place behind my station.

As I lined up my ingredients for the final round, I caught sight of Jordan across the room, setting up his station with the same methodical focus I remembered. There was a calmness to the way he handled each item, moving with a purpose that seemed to cut right through the tension in the room. I knew that look — that quiet intensity — and it sent an odd flutter through me, half-respect, half-resentment.

My stomach twisted as I watched him. Here he was, just as composed as ever, completely in his element. Meanwhile, I was fighting to keep my nerves in check and trying not to look like I'd gone twelve rounds with my purse. A small flicker of jealousy rose, and I immediately squashed it down.

Jordan might be the calmest chef in the room, but today, he was my biggest competitor. There was no time to get distracted by his cool confidence or the memories of the last time we'd both stood side by side in a competition kitchen.

But I couldn't help it. Watching him slide a cutting board into place and set up his knife like it was an extension of his hand, I was reminded of how much I'd admired his skill once. And, okay, fine, maybe still did. Jordan knew his way around a kitchen with an ease that few people did.

I shook my head, pulling myself back to the task at hand.

This wasn't the time for reminiscing.

We were rivals now, both fighting for more than just a win. I knew what it meant for me. But for him? Well, who knew?

What I did know was he'd have to pry this victory from my cold, bruised, concealer-caked hands.

With one last glance in his direction, I squared my shoulders. I would not let Jordan — or my feelings — distract me. Not today.

The announcer's voice rang out through the venue, igniting the already buzzing crowd. "Ladies and gentlemen, welcome to the *Whisk It All* finals!" Celeste Moretti, the show's host, leaned forward with a beaming smile. "After some tough competition, we're down to our final two chefs: Annie McGowan and Jordan Shaw! Can we get a huge round of applause for these culinary warriors?"

The audience erupted, filling the room with claps, cheers, and even a few hollers. My heart pounded, adrenaline mingling with nerves. I took a deep breath, gripping my station's edge as Celeste worked up the crowd even more.

"And now, the moment you've all been waiting for," Celeste continued. "Let's meet our special guest judges! First up, we have the queen of Southern cuisine, Chef Deidra Matthews!"

The applause rose even louder. Deidra Matthews, elegant with her signature silver bob, gave a gracious wave. Just the thought of her tasting my food sent a fresh jolt of nerves through me.

"Next, we have the fusion cuisine master himself, Chef Takeshi Mori!"

Takeshi, in a sleek black jacket, nodded with his usual laser-focused expression, and the audience clapped harder. His critiques were as precise as his knife skills—meaning he could slice my dish to pieces with a single comment.

"And finally," Celeste finished, "we have the queen of avant-garde desserts, Chef Luna Park!"

The crowd practically exploded. Luna, with her purple-streaked hair and eccentric style, flashed a peace sign to the crowd, her popularity almost palpable. My stomach churned. The final panel was serious.

Just as I was gathering myself, I heard Jordan's voice. "Good luck, Annie."

I turned, and he was standing close, the confidence he usually wore softened by an unexpected warmth in his eyes. "Really, I mean it."

I felt my cheeks flush, but managed a smile. "Thanks, Jordan. You too."

His expression softened as his gaze drifted, noticing the bruise peeking through the hopeless concealer. His brows knit in worry.

"What happened?" he asked, his tone shifting instantly to concern. He stepped forward… so close. I could smell the clean scent of his soap. I closed my eyes and just breathed it in. I almost didn't hear him ask, "Are you okay?"

I touched my cheek beneath my eye, feeling the heat rise in embarrassment. "Self inflicted," I said with a small laugh. "Tried bucking a fashion trend last night. I'm fine."

A flicker of worry lingered in his eyes. "You're sure?"

"Positive," I said, standing straighter, trying to brush it off.

For a brief moment, his hand lightly rested on my shoulder, his touch surprisingly comforting.

At that moment, Trent burst into the arena, and everyone's heads turned… including Jordan's. I saw the PA whisper conspiratorially to another PA.

Yeah. Forget my cooking.

My love life was the hot dish, apparently. Trent quickly pulled himself together and headed for the stands. He looked at me nervously, then I noticed him scanning the room… searching. A nagging worry prickled in my brain.

What had he meant? His father was rigging the competition.

"Hm," Jordan's assessment shook me from my reverie. "Well, looks you put up a fight, but I have a feeling you've got a lot more fight in you today."

I gave a determined nod. "Count on it."

With one last look, he returned to his station, leaving me feeling oddly steady, even as the nerves bubbled up again.

Chef Luna, today's lead judge, stepped forward, the tension thickening as her voice filled the room. "Welcome to the final round of *Whisk It All*," she announced. "Today's challenge is one that demands both respect for tradition and creative daring. Your task is to take a classic Italian dish and elevate it to new heights."

My pulse spiked, and I barely held back a smile. Italian cuisine was where I felt most at home, where my instincts were sharpest. It was my world, my passion, and now the stage was set for me to showcase it.

But right beside me, I felt Jordan's presence—steady, confident. A glance told me he was just as thrilled by the challenge, his expression intense with focus. Italian food meant something to both of us. He'd had his own journey with it, and I knew he wouldn't go easy.

The crowd watched, breathless, as the judge's words hung in the air, the magnitude of the challenge clear to everyone. Italian cuisine wasn't just food; it was love, tradition, history — each ingredient meant something deeper, each dish told a story. And this time, my story had to be bigger, bolder, and, hopefully, unforgettable.

My mind raced, flipping through classic recipes, and a swirl of ideas emerged, each more daring than the last. This wasn't just about taking a dish and giving it a few fancy twists.

No, I was here to pay homage to Vitello's, to the comforting, unpretentious flavors that made it a local gem, but with an edge that would wow these judges. I wanted every bite to be Vitello's at its heart — but bold enough to make them take notice.

The judge's countdown began, and with one last steadying breath, I picked up my knife, ready to bring everything I had to this plate. Italian food was my foundation.

And tonight, it was going to soar.

Chef Luna cleared her throat, pausing just before giving the final countdown. "And before we begin," she said, smiling at the cameras, "we have a very special guest joining our panel today."

The breath I'd just taken caught in my

throat.

Luna gestured toward the judges' table as a familiar figure strode onto the competition floor.

Charles Parker.

My heart slammed against my ribs.

Trent's father—the man who had spent his entire career pulling strings behind the scenes, who viewed people as assets and outcomes to be managed—was sitting at the judging table.

I swallowed hard.

He wasn't just here. He was going to be judging my food.

The murmur through the crowd barely registered. I felt frozen in place, my fingers tightening around my knife like it was the only thing keeping me upright.

Next to me, Jordan stiffened, no doubt sensing the shift in my energy. I could almost feel his gaze on me, but I couldn't tear my eyes away from the one person I had hoped never to see again.

This wasn't just about winning anymore.

This was about not letting Charles Parker decide my fate.

The cameras zoomed in, capturing the moment, but my mind was already spinning. Trent had tried to warn me—this was his warning. And I'd ignored him.

Chef Luna smiled. "With his unparalleled

expertise in the culinary business, Mr. Parker brings a keen eye for excellence."

Yeah. Excellence — and control.

The countdown resumed.

I exhaled sharply, forcing myself to focus.

This was my moment. My food. My fight.

And I refused to let Charles Parker pin me to the mat.

Chapter Twenty-Six

Jordan

Parker.

As in Trent Parker, Annie's fiancé.

My pulse kicked up a notch, but not out of excitement.

I should have been the one panicking. If Annie's fiancé's father was on the judging panel, then what chance did I have? This was a stacked deck if I'd ever seen one. Maybe she'd known all along. Maybe that's why she looked so calm—so sure of herself.

But then I really looked at her.

And my stomach twisted.

She looked… pale. Not the *Oh damn, this just got complicated* kind of pale. No, this was something else. Something closer to dread.

What the hell?

She had every reason to be celebrating this moment. Instead, she was gripping the edge of her station like she needed the countertop to hold her upright.

Something wasn't right.

I squared my shoulders. My jaw worked. Who cares? I can do this. I wasn't about to let some big-shot judge shake me. But as I prepped my station, my mind kept circling back to Annie. This guy had her nervous — and not in the healthy, competitive way.

And that? That bothered the hell out of me.
Focus, Shaw!
But Annie was all I could think about.

I took a deep breath, running through my options. Saltimbocca alla Romana — it was a challenge, bold and unforgiving, but if I pulled it off, the judges wouldn't forget it. It was a recipe that practically demanded perfection, and I wanted to bring out that burst of flavor in every bite, refined and unforgettable.

But even as I mentally sketched the deconstructed version in my head, something kept tugging at the edges of my thoughts, something that had nothing to do with cooking.
Annie's black eye.
She'd brushed it off with a joke, claiming she'd bucked some fashion trend. Sure, Annie had a knack for making even her clumsiest moments sound deliberate, but this seemed... off. And the more I thought about it, the less convinced I was that she'd just hit her face on accident.

I clenched my jaw. It was impossible not to think about Trent, wondering if he'd had something to do with it. The thought stirred something fierce in me, something protective.

If Trent had hurt her…

"Jordan!" A voice pulled me back to the present. I turned to find the emcee sidling up beside me, her bright smile nearly blinding. "So, word on the floor is you're preparing Saltimbocca alla Romana," she purred, clearly waiting for a response that would charm the viewers. "Bold choice. Tell the audience a little about it."

"Uh, yeah," I nodded, barely breaking stride, my thoughts still partly with Annie. "Saltimbocca means 'jump in the mouth.'"

The emcee's eyes sparkled, and she raised her brows with a flirtatious grin. "Oh, I'd like to see that."

I blinked, still caught between my dish and my worries about Annie. The flirtatious line sailed right past me. I managed a polite smile, but nothing more, and the emcee rolled her eyes, giving me a playful shrug before moving on to her next victim.

With a sigh, I redirected my focus, narrowing in on the plan forming in my mind. I wanted to take the classic saltimbocca—delicate veal, fragrant sage, that perfect slice of prosciutto—and turn it into something both elegant and surprising. Instead of wrapping and rolling the ingredients traditionally, I envisioned layers, each element deconstructed but harmonizing together. Something that would feel like an adventure with every bite but still hit with that unmistakable saltimbocca punch.

I shot a quick glance at Annie, and she was in her own world, every move of her knife controlled, her face lit with purpose. There was no distraction, no hesitation on her part. She was here for Vitello's, and I felt that weight settle on my shoulders.

But I was here for something important, too.

And that pushed me to bring my best to the table.

I glanced over at Annie's station again, my curiosity getting the better of me. She was focused, her hands moving quickly but precisely, gathering pasta and rich, earthy ingredients. Then it hit me.

Timballo di Maccheroni.

A twist tightened in my stomach as I realized what she was aiming for—an Italian classic that brought depth and simplicity together yet had the power to sweep anyone off their feet if executed right.

Timballo wasn't just any pasta dish. It was ambitious and comforting, a recipe that Italian grandmothers and fine-dining chefs alike revered for its balance of texture and flavor.

Knowing Annie, she would build each layer with intention, her brow furrowed in concentration, the whole thing looking almost too easy for her. If she pulled it off, this dish wouldn't just taste amazing; it'd feel like a hug straight from the heart of Italy.

A flicker of intimidation hit me. I couldn't deny it — Annie's culinary chops were on full display. She wasn't playing around. For a moment, a crack of doubt wormed its way into my confidence.

But then I straightened, adjusting my stance. I was here for a reason, and I was capable of greatness, too. Saltimbocca alla Romana wasn't a dish you took on lightly, but if I got it right, it would be every bit as memorable as her Timballo.

Maybe more.

Setting my focus back on my station, I took a steadying breath. This round wasn't just about Annie or me or any personal stakes. This was about being the best chef I knew I could be, about proving — to myself as much as anyone else — that I deserved this win.

As the timer started, the kitchen erupted into a controlled chaos, both of us moving with purpose and urgency. I reached for the veal, feeling the pressure of the clock with every beat of my pulse. Saltimbocca alla Romana wasn't just a dish — it was a feat of discipline and timing. I had to slice the veal perfectly thin, the meat delicate enough to melt with a sear, yet robust enough to hold the flavors of sage and prosciutto.

My knife flashed as I worked through the veal, measuring each slice with an obsessive eye for detail. Prosciutto followed, wafer-thin ribbons cut to complement each veal portion, then fresh sage—its scent sharp and earthy, grounding me in my task. I was hyper-aware of every second ticking by, the margin for error so small it felt like a thread. Even the sage leaves had to be carefully selected—too small and they'd overpower the bite, too large and they'd mask the balance.

At the next station, Annie was in her own rhythm, chopping and layering ingredients for her Timballo. It wasn't lost on me how ambitious her choice was—every part of a Timballo required intense focus, from preparing the ragu to cooking the pasta to the delicate layering of cheeses and filling. She was working with a near-poetic intensity, as if each piece of macaroni carried the weight of her entire life. I could see her placing each component as though the dish itself was a conversation with her past, her heritage, even her dreams. It was beautiful—and intimidating.

I turned back to my station, pushing thoughts of her aside. This dish, Saltimbocca, was every bit as intricate. First came the assembly, each slice of veal seasoned and topped with a layer of sage and prosciutto. With one swift motion, I secured each piece with a toothpick, my fingers moving with practiced efficiency. Then I turned to the pan, heating a precise amount of olive oil until it shimmered. Timing was everything here. I slid the first piece in, the sizzle immediate, filling the air with the intoxicating aroma of sage and meat.

Across from me, Annie poured sauce into her Timballo mold, her hands steady despite the tension in the room. Her dish required the same level of attention and finesse as mine, though her process was slower, every layer like a brick in an architectural masterpiece. The ragu bubbled softly. The macaroni absorbed its flavors, the cheeses melting and binding each piece together. I could tell she was creating something warm and rich, something that felt like home.

I shook my head, refocusing on my own process. I turned each Saltimbocca piece, caramelizing the edges just enough for a golden crust. This was a dish you couldn't rush, but you couldn't stall, either. The prosciutto had to crisp, but not too much. The sage needed to perfume the meat without overpowering it. A split-second too long, and I'd lose everything I was aiming for.

As I plated each piece of saltimbocca, laying them out with delicate sprigs of sage and a hint of reduced white wine sauce, the thought hit me like a slap to the face. Winning this competition would mean everything professionally.

I stopped.

But what did I risk losing?

I looked over to Annie's station, full lips in a concentrated pout... lips I longed to kiss again. Her red curls bounced with every step... curls I longed to tangle my fingers in.

Damn it!

If she could only see past her stubborn pride and anger, see how much this meant to me—not just the competition, but her.

The buzzer sounded. "And that's time, folks! Let's see what the judges think!" Celeste announced.

As the judges moved past Annie's station, I caught snippets of their murmured commentary. They leaned in close to her Timballo, inhaling the rich aroma of her ragu, the toasted breadcrumbs, the savory blend of cheeses.

Takeshi Mori, a stern-faced man known for his blunt honesty, murmured something, nodding slowly, his face unreadable. My pulse quickened as I strained to hear.

Then it came—

"A revelation," he said. The words hung in the air, heavy and unmistakable.

My stomach twisted, a pang of anxiety breaking through the steady calm I'd forced myself into. Annie's flavors, the simplicity she'd leaned into, were being met with nothing short of admiration. I could see her at her station, her face a mix of nerves and pride as she watched the judges savor every bite, appreciating her vision and skill.

Chef Luna chimed in, her voice low but clear. "This is true Italian comfort elevated. It brings a warmth, a memory, something beyond flavor." Her words trailed off as she exchanged looks with the other judges, each of them nodding in agreement.

I swallowed hard, tightening my grip on the utensils as I continued to plate my dish, but their comments echoed in my head. My Saltimbocca was a work of technique, of precision, carefully curated flavors.

But Annie's dish? It was something else entirely. It wasn't just food—it was heart on a plate. And it felt like she'd somehow taken everything I was trying to prove and distilled it into something beautiful, something undeniable.

I clenched my jaw, pushing down the anxiety that flared up at the edges of my focus. This was Annie's moment, her creation, and the judges were clearly moved by it.

But then it was Charles Parker's turn.

The tension in the room shifted the moment Charles Parker stepped forward.

He didn't rush. He never rushed. Men like

him never had to. He moved with the slow, deliberate precision of someone who had always been in control.

The lights above gleamed against his immaculate, custom-tailored suit, every movement crisp, calculated. He didn't bother glancing at the cameras. His presence alone commanded the room.

The other judges had taken their turns with technical critique and thoughtful praise. But Charles Parker? He was playing a different game altogether.

He was enjoying this.

I could see it in the way his mouth curled ever so slightly, in the deliberate pause as he picked up his fork.

He stared down at Annie's dish with mild disinterest, like he was inspecting a minor stock acquisition, not a carefully crafted plate of food. A dismissal so smooth it could cut without a single word.

Then he finally spoke.

"I suppose I expected something a little more… sophisticated," he mused, his voice laced with quiet disappointment, like a teacher marking up a failed assignment. Then, after a deliberate pause: "But I suppose there's a certain… rustic charm to it."

I saw Annie stiffen.

She was still. *Too still.*

Her expression was neutral, but her fingers flexed at her sides, a telltale sign she was barely holding herself together.

I clenched my jaw, my grip tightening on the edge of my station.

This wasn't about the food at all.

It was about control.

Charles Parker wasn't judging Annie's dish. He was reminding her exactly who held the power in this room. Annie shrank back.

And I hated that it seemed to be working.

Annie shouldn't have to shrink under this guy's scrutiny. She was better than that. Better than him.

I wanted to tell her that. Hell, I wanted to throw my own damn knife into the conversation.

My lips parted.

But then…

"That's enough."

The voice rang out sharp — cutting.

The entire room froze.

Including Charles Parker.

Chapter Twenty-Seven

Trent

The words left my mouth before I even fully processed them.

"That's enough!"

The sound sliced through the air like a whip crack.

The clatter of silverware, the murmur of the audience, the hum of cameras—everything stopped.

Cameras swiveled. Heads snapped toward me. Gasps rippled through the audience like a shockwave.

The floor felt suddenly too small, the heat of the stage lights pressing against my skin as I strode forward. Every step rang too loud in the silence.

The judges froze. The contestants stood stiff, eyes wide, uncertain whether this was part of the show or something wildly, irreversibly off-script.

Annie.

She was staring at me. Her lips slightly

parted, hands white-knuckled on the edge of her station. I couldn't read her expression — shock? Anger? Something deeper?

And then there was him.

Charles Parker didn't flinch.

Didn't even move.

He simply set down his fork with a deliberate, controlled motion, like he had all the time in the world. Like my presence was an inconvenience at best.

His gaze met mine, cold and unreadable.

But I saw it. That flicker.

Annoyance.

Good.

I wasn't done yet.

I didn't hesitate.

I didn't stop.

I didn't look at the cameras, the audience, or the stunned faces of the judges.

My focus was locked on one man.

Charles Parker.

My father.

Each step toward him felt heavier than the last, but I didn't falter. This was it. The moment I'd spent my whole life avoiding. The moment I could finally break free.

The polished floor beneath me felt like a battlefield, every stride a declaration of war. My pulse pounded in my ears, but my hands were steady. For the first time in my life, I wasn't walking in his shadow. I was walking toward it— ready to tear it down.

The audience didn't breathe. The cameras tracked my every movement. The producers? Frozen, panicked, unsure if they should intervene.

I didn't care.

This wasn't about them.

This was about her.

Annie.

The woman I loved… and failed.

The woman my father thought he could manipulate like another pawn in his empire.

Not today. Not ever again.

I stopped just short of the judges' table, my voice steady, unwavering.

"You don't belong here," I hissed.

Charles finally looked up.

And I didn't back down.

My father didn't flinch.

He didn't jerk in surprise or demand I leave. He didn't so much as lift an eyebrow.

Instead, he simply paused.

Fork poised over Annie's dish, he remained perfectly still, as if my interruption was nothing more than an inconvenient commercial break. The tension in the room was suffocating, pressing in from all sides. The cameras zoomed in. The producers whispered frantically into headsets. But

Charles?

He stayed cool.

Too cool.

But I knew him.

I knew that slight flicker of his eyes, the near-imperceptible tightening of his jaw.

I'd rattled him.

Good.

He set the fork down with precision, the sound of silver against porcelain sharp in the silence. Then, finally, he looked at me.

Measured. Unbothered. Calculating.

"Trent." His voice was smooth, unhurried, controlled. "What exactly do you think you're doing?"

I clenched my fists. The sheer *audacity* of him.

He knew damn well what I was doing.

But he wanted to make me say it. To play his game.

I wasn't giving him the satisfaction.

I took a step closer, lowering my voice just enough to still make sure every mic in the room picked it up.

"Telling the truth." I pushed through. "You think you can do this, Dad?" My voice cut through the studio like a blade, sharp and unrelenting. "You think you can just control everything?"

The words hit like a slap, reverberating

through the stunned silence.

Charles didn't react—not visibly. But I saw it. That flicker in his eyes. That tiny, almost imperceptible hesitation. The cracks in his armor weren't obvious, but they were there.

One small step toward victory.

I took another step forward, voice steady but edged with barely contained fury. "That's what this is about, right? Not the competition. Not Annie's food. Not even me." I let my gaze sweep over the cameras, the audience, the other judges. "It's just another power play. Another way for you to remind everyone—" I pointed a sharp finger at him "—that nothing happens without your say-so."

A murmur rippled through the crowd. The producers should have cut the feed by now, but they didn't. They wouldn't.

Because they knew.

They knew a moment when they saw one.

I stared down the man who had dictated my entire life.

But not today.

Not anymore.

"You don't own this competition," I said, my voice steady. "And you sure as hell don't own me."

I turned to the cameras now, making sure the world—everyone—heard what I was about to say.

"You weren't supposed to be here, were you, Dad?" My voice carried across the set, over the hushed crowd, straight to the man who had spent his life pulling strings from the shadows. "You weren't on the original judging panel. You didn't get this spot because of your expertise." I let the words sink in. "You bought your way onto this panel."

Gasps rippled through the audience.

Charles still didn't flinch, his grip tightening around his fork. But I saw the way his jaw ticked. The way his fingers curled just slightly.

Gotcha.

I didn't stop. "You pulled strings at the last second, used every connection you had, just so you could sit there and pretend to judge fairly." I let the silence drag before delivering the final blow. "And why? Not because you give a damn about this competition. Not because you care about food. But because you wanted to make sure Annie didn't win."

The crowd erupted. Producers scrambled. The cameras zoomed in on my father's face, the carefully curated mask of Charles Parker III cracking at the edges.

I stepped forward, voice firm. "Out of sheer spite."

I didn't come unarmed.

Reaching into my pocket, I pulled out my phone, the screen already lit with the email. The proof.

Bet he was regretting giving me an all-access pass to internal communiqué right about now.

"Let's not pretend this is some misunderstanding," I said, my voice cutting through the chaos. I turned the screen toward the cameras, ensuring every single person in the room—and every viewer at home—saw what I had in my hands.

A forwarded email chain. A timestamp. Receipts.

"Here it is. An email from your assistant, confirming your last-minute addition to the judges' panel." I scrolled. "And here—an internal memo about ensuring 'certain contestants' don't proceed to the final round." I lifted my gaze, pinning my father with a look that could cut glass. "Go ahead, Dad. Tell me again how this is just business."

The audience erupted. Gasps. Shouts. A ripple of disbelief spread through the room.

The cameras zoomed in. The producers didn't dare cut the feed.

Charles Parker's face remained eerily controlled, but I saw it—that flash of something in his eyes. That tiny, almost imperceptible flicker of panic.

I had him.

And for the first time in my life, I was the one pulling the strings.

"This isn't a business deal, Dad. You can't buy this win."

My voice was steady, but the weight behind it was a battering ram. Deliberate. Unshakable. I wasn't the same son he could silence with a look. Not anymore.

Charles's expression barely shifted — barely — but I saw it. The twitch of his jaw. The subtle curl of his fingers tightening around his fork. He was holding on, clinging to control like a man dangling from a fraying rope.

"You're making a spectacle of yourself, Trent." His voice was calm, practiced — too practiced. The Parker brand of damage control.

I took a step closer, closing the space between us. "No, I'm making sure the world sees exactly who you are." My chest rose and fell with controlled fury. "For once, you don't get to dictate the outcome."

The room held its breath.

The mask was slipping. And I was going to rip it off completely.

I turned to Annie.

The fury still burned in my chest, but as I looked at her — stunned, motionless, her hands gripping the edge of her station — I felt something else crash over me. Regret. Clarity. The weight of everything I hadn't said. The choices I hadn't made. The moments I had let slip through my fingers.

I took a breath, steadying myself. No more excuses. No more standing in the shadows while my father dictated my life.

"Annie," I said, my voice raw, stripped of all pretense. "I should have fought for you sooner. I should have stood up to him before. But I'm doing it now. And I don't care what it costs me."

Her lips parted slightly, but she didn't speak. She just stared, her green eyes wide, searching.

"I love you," I said, voice strong—clear. "But I know I don't deserve someone like you. I have some work to do on myself first. And I'm going to start by not letting my father take this from you."

The silence shattered.

Gasps. Cheers. The audience exploded. Reporters scrambled for their notebooks. A headline was being written in real-time. Cameras zoomed in, capturing every flicker of emotion on Annie's face.

And Charles Parker?

For the first time in my life, he had nothing to say.

Chapter Twenty-Eight

Annie

The world felt too loud and too quiet all at once.

The cameras were on me. The audience was watching, waiting for my reaction. But my brain couldn't catch up.

Trent's words still hung in the air, reverberating through my entire body. *I love you. But I know I don't deserve someone like you.*

I gripped the edge of my station, trying to steady myself. My heart pounded, my breath shallow, my pulse a frantic drum against my ribs. The heat from the stage lights felt suffocating, the weight of a hundred staring eyes pressing in from all sides.

Charles Parker stood rigid, his carefully composed mask beginning to crack. The murmurs of the audience escalated into a buzz of disbelief. The cameras were relentless, capturing every flicker of his reaction.

Then a voice rang out.

"Mr. Parker, you need to come with us."

Two competition officials stepped forward, their polished professionalism barely masking the fact that *this was huge.* This wasn't just a scandal — it was a public execution of his reputation.

Charles didn't stand immediately. Instead, he exhaled sharply, slow and controlled, adjusting his cuffs like *he* was the one calling the shots.

But no one was buying it.

"I'll be making a statement," he said coolly.

No one cared.

Another murmur rippled through the crowd as a producer whispered something frantically into a headset. Then, from somewhere in the press pit, a reporter muttered just loud enough to be overheard, "Parker stock's already taking a hit."

Another one scoffed. "Eating at a Parker restaurant is about to be considered truly 'bad taste.'"

Charles must've heard it, but he didn't react. Not visibly, at least. Just clenched his jaw and walked off the stage, his security detail falling into step beside him.

The audience *erupted.*

Applause, whispers, gasps. The energy in the room shifted so violently it made my head spin. The remaining judges exchanged stunned looks, conversing in hushed tones in the corner. The production crew scrambled, and reporters were already typing headlines at lightning speed.

And Trent?

Trent was still standing there.

His chest rose and fell in controlled breaths, but there was something different in his stance. Lighter—like the weight of a lifetime had just been lifted off his shoulders.

He turned toward me, the chaos fading into the background.

And then it was just us.

For the first time in what felt like forever, I saw *him*. Not Charles Parker's son. Not the guy who played by the rules. Not the man who let his father dictate every step of his life.

Just Trent.

And it broke something in me.

"Trent…" My voice barely made it past my lips. There was too much to say. Too much I didn't have words for.

He shook his head. "You don't have to say anything."

I searched his face, looking for regret, for pain—*for hope.* But all I found was peace.

And maybe, just maybe, a little of closure.

A small, self-deprecating smile played on his lips. "Guess I finally figured out how to stand up for something, huh?"

I let out a breathy laugh, but my throat was tight. "Yeah. You did."

A pause stretched between us, thick with things unsaid.

Then, quieter, softer, Trent said, "You deserve someone who's always been sure about you. Don't waste time waiting for them to say it."

My breath caught.

Because I knew exactly what he meant.

And so did he.

My lips parted, but I couldn't find the words.

Trent just smiled. Not bitter. Not sad. Just… *accepting.*

Then, with one last glance — one last moment — he turned and stepped off the stage.

And just like that, I knew.

It was over.

And maybe, for the first time since all of this started… I was really free.

My chest rose and fell in uneven breaths as I watched Trent walk away. The noise of the crowd was still a dull roar in my ears, but my focus drifted — past the flashing cameras, past the murmuring judges — until it landed on him.

Jordan.

He was still at his station, standing stock-still, his hands braced against the counter like he needed something solid to hold on to. His dark eyes weren't on Trent. Weren't on the spectacle unraveling around them.

They were on me.

And what I saw there sent a fresh wave of warmth through her chest.

He wasn't gloating. He wasn't smirking. He wasn't waiting for the dust to settle so he could swoop in and stake his claim.

He was just... watching.

Like he wanted to make sure I was okay.

Like he'd been waiting for me to choose — but had never once considered forcing my hand.

But I was still raw.

I didn't know if I was ready to choose anything.

No. That wasn't true. There was still Vitello's.

At the judges' table, Celeste Moretti cleared her throat, tapping a manicured nail against the microphone. The sound crackled through the speakers, snapping the room back into focus.

"Alright, chefs," she said, her voice smooth, practiced — commanding. "We acknowledge the... unexpected turn of events today, but let me be clear — this competition is still happening."

A murmur rippled through the crowd. My pulse jumped.

Moretti folded her hands on the table, looking directly at me, then Jordan. "The integrity of Whisk It All remains intact. The judging will proceed fairly. No manipulation. No interference." She let that hang in the air before adding, "So, if anyone was hoping to win on a technicality… think again."

Her gaze swept across the stage, waiting for anyone to object.

No one did.

I swallowed hard. My fingers curled into fists at my sides.

This wasn't over.

I still had a competition to win

Chapter Twenty-Nine

Jordan

I couldn't shake the feeling that I was standing on the edge of something monumental.

The competition. The moment I'd been working toward. The thing I'd poured everything into. And yet, all I could think about was *her*.

Annie.

She stood only a few feet away, but it felt like miles. The air between us crackled, charged with something bigger than this competition—something neither of us had the time or space to unpack.

Because Trent Parker had just blown up his entire world.

And hers.

And mine.

I swallowed hard, trying to push through the storm in my chest. I should have been relieved. Trent had stepped aside, made it clear that he wasn't the guy for her.

But instead of feeling like I had a clear shot,

I just felt... unsettled.

Because what if, after everything, she wasn't ready for anyone?

What if she still wasn't ready for me?

The judges were coming. I squared my shoulders, forcing myself to focus. Whatever happened next, I had to win.

Everything was riding on it.

And Annie had no idea.

As the judges finally arrived at my station, I held my breath, every muscle taut. This was the moment I'd poured every ounce of myself into, crafting each element of the Saltimbocca with painstaking care. I glanced down at my dish, a vision of carefully seared veal with translucent prosciutto draped over it, the sage leaves crisped to perfection, and a glossy reduction sauce pooling just right on the plate.

Chef Luna leaned in, examining each element with a meticulous eye. I could feel my pulse racing as she cut a piece, her fork lingering for an excruciating second before she took the first bite. The others followed suit, tasting in silence, their expressions unreadable.

Finally, the judge on the left, Deidra Matthews—a Southern belle notorious for her sharp tongue—glanced up, her brows lifting ever so slightly. "The balance of flavors here is...exquisite," she said, her voice a touch softer than usual. "The prosciutto melds with the veal seamlessly, and the sage—subtle but unmistakable." She gave a small nod of approval, and I felt a glimmer of hope spark.

Chef Luna took a second bite, savoring it with slow deliberation. "Your execution is razor sharp, Jordan. This dish respects tradition but adds a refined edge. And the presentation? Impeccable."

Relief seeped in, but the last judge, Takeshi, with years of experience behind him, remained stoic, his gaze fixed on me. "It's technically flawless," he said, his voice gruff but sincere. "You've done justice to the Saltimbocca, no question."

I nodded, feeling a deep sense of pride tempered with lingering nerves. I'd achieved what I set out to do. But with Annie's dish already hailed as a revelation, I knew I still had everything to prove.

To her…

Then it came. The moment of truth.

The judges gathered at their table, heads bent together as they murmured in quiet, intense deliberation. My heartbeat pounded in my ears as Annie and I stood side by side, both of us bracing ourselves for the verdict. She was right there, her hands clasped in front of her, brow furrowed with that focused determination I knew so well. If it weren't for the stakes—and the crowd, and the judges, and…everything—I would've turned to her, cracked a joke, anything to relieve the suffocating tension.

But this was it. After all these years, every choice, every sacrifice, every setback, every damn step had led here.

Takeshi gestured emphatically toward our stations, his hand lingering over mine, then sweeping toward Annie's. Luna Park leaned in, whispering something I couldn't quite catch, but her nod told me it was serious, like they were debating more than just flavor profiles. Maybe heart, soul—whatever part of us we'd infused into these plates.

I chanced another glance at Annie, who caught my eye, her face a mix of nerves and something deeper—maybe a shadow of the old fire between us. Then she looked away, jaw set. This was as much about our history as it was about winning, and the realization twisted something inside me, a pull of regret, hope, and…

"Chefs, please step forward," Luna called, her voice ringing with authority.

The room held its breath. I glanced at Annie again, feeling every inch of the distance between us.

Luna looked down her pointed nose, her gaze steady, serious. "This year's Whisk It All champion," she began, letting the suspense hang in the air, "is…"

Chapter Thirty

Annie

The head judge stepped forward, her gaze sweeping over us, her expression solemn yet triumphant, as if she knew exactly the weight of this moment. I held my breath, my fingers crossed so tightly they ached. This was it. I'd thrown everything I had into that Timballo, every ounce of skill, determination, every memory of Vitello's — the sound of Louie's laugh, the smell of garlic mingling with fresh basil, the laughter that filled that tiny dining room on its best nights. This competition was my last chance to preserve it all.

The judge drew out the silence, savoring it. "This year's Whisk It All champion," she began, her words hanging like the last notes of an opera, "is…Jordan Murphy!"

Applause erupted from the crowd, but it barely registered. My heart sank, the weight of disappointment settling in hard and fast. I forced myself to clap along, reminding myself this was good news for Jordan. He'd earned it. I couldn't deny that. He was talented. He deserved this. But it didn't make the loss sting any less.

As the crowd's cheers swelled, I caught sight of him across the room. His face lit up with the realization of victory. He looked... so alive, so proud, so Jordan. I knew I should feel happy for him, and part of me did. But as the applause continued, my mind drifted back to Vitello's, to Louie, to everything that was now in jeopardy.

Forcing a smile, I clapped a little harder, hoping no one noticed the ache that had crept in beneath my enthusiasm. This was his moment. And, I reminded myself, I'd just have to find another way to save my home.

The applause felt like a distant hum, muffled by the thud of disappointment settling in my chest. Jordan's grin was infectious, his energy lighting up the stage as he accepted the award. I clapped along, forcing a smile, even as I felt the pangs of regret gnawing at me. This was his moment, and he'd earned it, fair and square. But knowing how close I'd come, how much I'd wanted to win for Vitello's, was like a stone lodged in my throat.

The thought of Louie's face flashed in my mind, his warm grin fading into the uncertainty that had hovered around us all month. I'd wanted this so badly — for the restaurant, for everything that Vitello's meant. But it looked like my grand plan had just hit a serious speed bump.

Okay. Maybe more like Mount Everest.

I took a deep breath, forcing myself to stand a little straighter. This wasn't the end. Sure, it felt like the door had just slammed shut in my face, but there were other doors, right? I'd find another way. This place, these people, meant too much to let go. The flicker of determination I'd come in with hadn't been snuffed out completely — it just needed some coaxing.

I watched Jordan as he left the stage, catching his eye. His victory smile softened, and for a second, I thought he was going to walk over. My heart skipped in that ridiculous way it did around him, even now, despite everything. But then the crowd surged forward, cutting between us, and he disappeared into a sea of congratulatory pats on the back.

"Okay, universe," I muttered to myself, "you got me this time. But let's see what you throw my way next."

I stood back, folding my arms as Jordan was swarmed by the judges, other chefs, and well-wishers. The genuine joy on his face as he talked animatedly, hands flying to emphasize his excitement, was infectious. It was the Jordan I remembered from years ago — alive, thriving, in his element. The sight tugged at me, bringing a smile to my face that I didn't quite expect, even as my disappointment lingered.

He'd earned this, no question. Watching him now, seeing the way he lit up, I couldn't help but feel a flash of pride. This was the man I'd fallen for once upon a time, back when dreams were simpler and plans didn't involve corporate mergers or desperate last-ditch competitions. Back when food wasn't just about winning but about sharing a piece of yourself on a plate.

I caught his eye from across the room, and he smiled, a genuine, slightly softened smile that seemed to acknowledge everything that had passed between us, even in its silence. For a second, I wondered what might have happened if things had gone differently — if he hadn't won that first competition, if I hadn't left, if...

Well, if a lot of things.

But as quickly as the thought settled in, the sting of reality pulled me back. Winning had been my chance to save Vitello's, and now... that chance was gone. And even though I was happy for him, seeing Jordan in the spotlight reminded me of the sacrifices I'd made, the relentless pursuit of a dream that had nearly pushed me away from everything I cared about.

I wanted to believe there was still a way forward, even without the prize, but a nagging doubt crept in, mingling with the bittersweet pride I felt for him.

As the crowd thinned, I lingered, my hands still gripping the edge of the counter. I looked around at the competition arena, thinking about what this journey had cost me—late nights, early mornings, all the times I'd felt like I was barely holding on by a thread. And for what?

To save a restaurant I adored?

Yes.

To prove I could go the distance?

Abso-freakin-lutely.

But lately, my dream had been so tangled up in other people's expectations, reshaped by Trent's ambitions and warped by everyone else's notions of who I should be.

I glanced over at Jordan one last time as he laughed with the judges, basking in his victory. And instead of feeling envy, I felt something softer, lighter—clarity, maybe. I'd lost, sure, but watching him, I realized I didn't need a trophy or the spotlight to confirm my worth. I'd put my heart into this, just as I'd put my heart into Vitello's every single day, and that was validation enough. The thrill of cooking, the satisfaction of a well-made dish, the joy of creating something from nothing—that was why I did this. That was my reward, my fuel.

And for the first time, I allowed myself to believe that my dreams weren't dependent on anyone else's approval. They didn't rely on grand gestures or life-altering wins. They were right here, every time I stepped into a kitchen, every time I plated a meal with care. All I needed was my dedication, my passion to keep going.

With a deep breath, I felt a weight lift, and for the first time in a long time, I knew exactly what I was fighting for—my dream, my way—and that was more powerful than any prize.

As the realization settled in, I felt something shift inside me, like a puzzle piece sliding into place.

Yes, winning would have been amazing—game-changing, even. But was it the only way to save Vitello's? Watching the last of the spectators drift out, I thought of our regulars, the people who showed up week after week, as loyal to the restaurant as they were to each other. The soul of Vitello's wasn't in shiny awards or titles. It was in every perfectly cooked dish that had brought comfort, every laugh shared over a meal. The strength of our little restaurant came from the community that supported it and the passion that fueled us.

Our strength…

"Is love," I whispered to myself.

Maybe there was another way to rally the people who loved Vitello's, a way to make them part of its story again.

All those hours I'd spent worrying,

stressing over a competition win, I'd been looking for a single solution when, really, Vitello's wasn't a restaurant that needed one big moment to save it. It just needed the steady heartbeats of those with dedication and love for the place. The heart and soul Louie and I put into every dish, every shift, every time I set foot in that kitchen — that was the true strength, and I could trust in it.

I took a deep breath, letting the weight of the competition melt away. I might have lost the title, but I hadn't lost my vision for Vitello's. If anything, I felt more determined than ever.

The only catch?

Time.

The bank's looming deadline wouldn't wait for me to dawdle.

I fiddled with Trent's engagement ring, the ostentatious, four-carat rock he had insisted on putting on my hand. I had forgotten to take it off after last night's debacle. I hadn't even taken it off for the competition. He refused to let me remove it throughout our entire engagement — insisting it showed everyone just how much he loved me. I scowled.

You mean, how much money his father had.

I mean, really. Who in the hell spent $50,000 on a damned ring? I started working it off my finger. And that's when it hit me.

Fifty…thousand…dollars.

I shook off any last doubts, straightened my shoulders, and felt an unexpected smile spread across my face. There was still a battle ahead, and I was ready for it.

But I had better move fast. Valentine's Day was tomorrow, and the clock was ticking

Chapter Thirty-One

Jordan

As the applause died down and people began drifting away, I scanned the room, looking for her. Annie. In the sea of faces and handshakes, all I wanted was to find her. Winning had been the goal, sure, but not for the reasons anyone here thought. This wasn't just a competition. This was my chance to show Annie—show her what I hadn't been able to put into words.

But she wasn't there.

A strange emptiness settled in. Not that I didn't appreciate the congratulations or the admiring glances from the other contestants. But as I shook their hands, I couldn't shake the feeling that none of it mattered without her. I'd built this moment around her, around what I'd wanted her to see—that I understood her dreams, that I wasn't just here for a trophy but for her.

The more I looked around, the more I hoped to see her, maybe lingering at the edges, waiting for me to notice her. For the last few weeks, I'd been walking a line, trying to prove something to her that went beyond apologies and words. I'd pictured her smile, her approval, the way she might look at me if she saw I'd gone all in for her. And now, it was just me, standing in a half-empty room, my goal met, but somehow, my victory hanging in the air like an unanswered question.

As people cleared out, that question grew louder in my mind: Had I pushed too hard, assumed too much? Winning had meant nothing if it didn't mean something to her.

I limped over to Celeste Moretti, hoping for a quick answer about Annie, but from the gleam in her eye, she was clearly reading this all wrong. She adjusted her mic and leaned in with a smile that was definitely less about the competition and more about something else.

"Well, well," she said, glancing down at my cast. "Finally coming around, huh? Thought maybe you'd want a little company after all that excitement. Or someone to play *nurse* for that leg?"

I forced a polite smile, not exactly in the mood. "Appreciate the offer, but I was just wondering if you'd seen Annie. She took off pretty quick, and I thought I saw her over here earlier."

Celeste tilted her head, pouting slightly. "Annie, huh?" She leaned back, tapping her chin thoughtfully. "Let's see. I thought I saw her around a few minutes ago, but you know, she wasn't exactly... lingering." She gave a little shrug. "Can't really blame her. Some people are just sore losers."

She let that hang for a second, studying my reaction, then finally nodded over toward the main exit. "Last I saw, she was headed that way. But she seemed... a little distracted."

"Thanks, Celeste." I kept it short, trying not to let my irritation show.

"Oh, don't mention it," she said, giving my shoulder a gentle squeeze. "Just holler if you need someone to give you a sponge bath!"

I thanked her with a nod, already moving away, but her words echoed in my mind.

Annie had been distracted. And she'd left without a word.

I wove through the backstage area, dodging handshakes, claps on the back, and enthusiastic congratulations from fellow chefs, but my mind was far from the win.

Each step felt heavier as the thought grew — Annie might have left before the last announcement, before I could find her. People were buzzing around me, congratulating me on the win, but it all faded into background noise.

I tried to keep my cool, but inside, frustration was brewing. Every handshake and grin just reminded me she wasn't here.

The whole point of this competition wasn't just about the trophy or the recognition; it was about Annie — proving to her I'd changed, that I could be the man she once believed in, the man she deserved. It was a minor miracle I hadn't gone hoarse talking myself up to every reporter, mentioning my motivations and passions, all with her in mind.

But here I was, clutching a win in one hand and an emptiness in the other.

People moved around me, chattering about the judges' praise and my so-called "refined creativity," as I took the longest route imaginable through the crowd, hoping for a glimpse of her face. She wouldn't just vanish — at least, I told myself she wouldn't. Annie wasn't one to shy away from offering an honest critique or sharing in someone else's moment. And it's not like her to leave loose ends untied, either.

But if she'd left, maybe I'd read this all wrong.

I gripped the edges of the award, feeling the cool metal dig into my fingers. All I wanted was one moment with her, a chance to share what I'd accomplished. But the thought of her walking out before the final applause even faded left a hollow ache that not even the taste of victory could fix.

I pulled out my phone, holding onto a

ridiculous hope that maybe Annie had texted me. A simple "congrats" or even a sarcastic "you showed me" would've been better than the nothing staring back at me. My screen was blank, save for the time ticking forward. It shouldn't have bothered me so much, but it did — more than I'd admit.

I scrolled through old messages — I'd never deleted a single one shed sent — past ones filled with all the teasing and challenging banter that'd kept us on our toes back when we were still Annie and Jordan. There'd been a time when our lives practically revolved around good food, late nights, and pushing each other to be better. I thought winning today might bring back a glimpse of those days. I wasn't looking to rewind, exactly, but I thought that maybe...

The longer I stared at the empty screen, the heavier it felt in my hand, and the realization hit — she'd probably left. She'd wanted to win for Vitello's, and with me taking the title, maybe it had been too much to watch.

Still, she'd been proud enough to congratulate me once...so why couldn't she do it now? I clenched my jaw, feeling a flash of resentment mixed in with the frustration. Annie had always been the one to push me to reach higher.

And all I wanted to do was take her with me.

My mind drifted, tugged back by a memory that lingered somewhere between nostalgia and regret. It was the Kansas State Fair, the night I had, technically, "stolen" the casserole competition win from Annie.

It had started as a playful challenge, something to keep us both sharp. We had been each other's biggest fans, pushing one another toward excellence. The night before the fair, we had been lolling in the hayloft at my family's farm. When I heard her talking about her Chicken Acapulco recipe, it sounded so amazing I knew it had a great chance of winning.

But why not double our chances?

No matter whose name the judges called, it would be a win. If Annie won, she'd get her down payment to open her own place. And if I won, he'd do the same… only I'd keep back just enough to buy a ring. And so, I entered with a similar recipe.

And then it all went up in smoke.

When they announced my name as the winner, I'll admit, I felt a surge of pride. People cheered and clapped that day, and the smell of fried food and fresh hay drifted through the fairgrounds, filling me with that intoxicating rush of achievement. I'd stood up there grinning like an idiot, hoping to catch her eye. But when I looked around, ready to share that moment with her, she was gone.

At first, I'd thought she was just dodging the crowd, maybe grabbing us a celebratory lemonade or funnel cake. But as the excitement settled, there was still no sign of her. The fair's energy pulsed around me — barkers calling out game prizes, children running past with sticky candy apples, and a country band playing upbeat tunes in the background. But I couldn't shake the unease that crept up my spine.

Finally, I made my way to Granny McGowan's house, clutching a small velvet box in my pocket, heavy with the weight of a promise I wanted to make. I'd squirreled away most of the prize money but kept enough to buy a ring I'd found at a nearby antique store. I could still see the ring in my mind — a simple but elegant band with a tiny stone that sparkled with the same warmth I saw in Annie's eyes.

I'd planned to ask her that night — lying in the hay, counting the stars through the hayloft door, where we had been talking about our dreams, our goals, about making a life together where we could both keep pushing toward greatness.

By the time I got to Granny Mc Gowan's, Granny had been sitting alone in her living room, knitting needles clacking softly, the air thick with the smell of apple pie cooling on the windowsill.

She glanced up with a knowing look, as if she had been waiting for me, and just shook her head slightly.

"She's gone, isn't she?" I'd asked, trying to keep my voice steady.

Granny McGowan nodded slowly, her needles stilling in her lap. "She left 'bout an hour ago, sugar. Said she needed to clear her head."

"Did she say why?"

"She didn't have to. Sometimes, when people don't feel seen, they go where they're sure they'll be missed." She patted the seat beside her, her gaze gentle but steady. "Now, why don't you tell me what's got you here with your heart all twisted up?"

I sat beside her, feeling my throat tighten as I looked down at the box in my hand. "I just... I had all these plans. Winning this contest, well, that was just a way to make them happen. I guess... I guess I just wasn't good enough for her."

Granny sighed, placing a warm, worn hand on mine. "Oh, honey. You've always had what it takes for Annie. She doesn't care about trophies or contests. What she needed was to feel like she was part of your journey, not just a stop along the way."

The words settled over him, uncomfortable and heavy, like a thick quilt in summer. I opened the box, showing Granny the ring I'd been

planning to give Annie. "I thought maybe…
maybe if she saw this, she'd know. That I wanted
her with me. That I'd always want her."

Granny peered at the ring, her mouth
curving into a soft smile tinged with sympathy.
"It's a beautiful ring, honey. But sometimes, love's
about more. It's about the everyday showing up—
making room. And Annie… she wants to build
something real, something that's as much hers as
it is yours."

I'd felt a pang of realization, but I tried to
shove it down. "I know that, Granny. I do. I
wanted to show her I was willing to give her
everything."

Granny squeezed his hand, a look of
wisdom shining in her eyes. "Everything except
the space she needed. She'll come back, you know.
But she'll need to know she's standing beside you,
not behind you."

As I stepped outside into the cool evening, I
looked around, hoping I'd see her just up ahead,
maybe hesitating by the street corner.

But the sidewalk was empty, save for a few
folks heading to their cars. Every second without
seeing her chipped away at my confidence. The
longer I stood there, the more I wondered if she
was gone for good.

Annie's apartment came to mind—the last
safe place for both of us in this tangled mess. I

pictured the small space, warm and familiar, with her shelves lined with cookbooks and that little stack of dog-eared recipe cards by the stovetop. She'd created a place filled with life and purpose. Somehow, that apartment felt more like home than any other place I'd known.

But not Annie.

Suddenly, I knew where she'd be. The surge of determination hit like a shot of espresso. She'd gone back to her own corner of the world, and I'd go there too, if it meant setting things right. If she was there, I'd finally say it all—the truth about why I entered this competition, about how none of it was worth a damn without her.

And if she still wanted to marry this Trent guy? Well, I wouldn't stand in the way.

Without thinking, I shoved my phone into my pocket and set my shoulders. This wasn't just about clearing things up; this was about showing her that every part of this—every decision I'd made—was because I wanted her in my life. I didn't have every answer she'd need, but I'd make sure she knew I was choosing her. I wasn't letting her walk out without knowing exactly what she meant to me.

Not this time.

Chapter Thirty-Two

Annie

The bell above the door tinkled as I stepped into the jeweler's shop, feeling as if I'd crossed the point of no return. The shop was quiet, the air a mix of polish and leather, with soft lights illuminating rows of shimmering jewels in glass cases.

Each ring, necklace, and bracelet sparkled with a kind of polish I'd only ever seen in magazine ads. I felt out of place, and I almost turned around, but I took a steadying breath and approached the counter, focusing on the task at hand.

A man with gentle, lined eyes and a neatly pressed suit stepped forward, his gaze drifting to the ring I held out. He looked up at me, his expression softening, as though he'd seen this scenario a hundred times before. "Good afternoon. How can I help you?"

I cleared my throat, feeling as if I needed an extra nudge to get the words out. "I... I'd like to sell this." My voice sounded firmer than I expected, though the words still felt strange. "It's, um, my engagement ring," I added quickly, feeling a hint of embarrassment. "Things just… didn't work out."

He nodded with an understanding smile that helped put me at ease. "It happens more often than you think." Taking the ring, he lifted it toward one of the soft lights, letting it catch every glimmer from the sparkling diamond. I watched him with my heart thudding, unsure if I wanted the ring to be worth a fortune or next to nothing. Each angle he inspected made me hold my breath. "Shame though. To happen on Valentine's Day."

You're telling me, mister.

Finally, after what felt like an eternity, he lowered the ring and looked at me with a small, gentle smile. "This is a fine piece. I can offer you a substantial sum." He named a figure that made me blink in surprise, my heart leaping slightly. It wasn't enough to cover Vitello's balloon payment completely, but it was a start. Enough to buy us some breathing room, to buy Louie just a little more time.

"Thank you," I murmured, my voice barely more than a whisper as relief washed over me. This wouldn't solve everything, but it was something—a step forward.

With the cash in my hand, I stepped back

out onto the street and broke into a near sprint, weaving through pedestrians, dodging a mother with a stroller, and half-apologizing to an older man whose cane I nearly kicked on accident.

My pulse hammered, and a strange cocktail of hope and dread swirled in my chest. I clutched the envelope, its weight oddly comforting in my hand as I pushed myself to go faster.

It was enough to buy us some time. Maybe not a lot, but enough. Just enough to hold off the bank and Trent's father — to breathe a little, to plot out the next steps together.

I pictured Louie's face as I burst through the doors at Vitello's, his bushy eyebrows lifting in surprise, his familiar grin breaking out as I handed him the money. The relief we'd share, the reassurance that we could save this place — the heartbeat of our neighborhood — together.

But with every step closer, another worry crept in, whispering that I might already be too late. The balloon payment was due so soon, and I'd watched Louie carry that weight alone, his silent resolve slipping only in those moments he thought no one noticed.

What if he'd already resigned himself to losing Vitello's? What if he'd found no other option than selling?

The thought twisted my stomach into knots, making my heart pound harder. I quickened my pace, willing myself to arrive in time. Everything felt charged, the surrounding city a blur as I focused on Vitello's. I could see the red neon sign just a block away, and a spark of hope flared within me.

This place was home, as much a part of me as my own dreams. I had to believe Louie would feel the same—had to believe he'd take this chance, however small, to fight with me.

I reached the restaurant, panting and grabbing at the painful stitch in my side.

Note to self… lay off the chocolate ice cream.

But I'd made it. I hoped. I stood outside Vitello's, catching my breath, the envelope still clutched tightly in my hand. For a moment, I just took in the familiar façade. The old, weathered sign above the door glowed with a soft red hue, and I could almost feel the energy of years past, the warmth that had kept this place alive even when the world outside had felt cold. This wasn't just a restaurant. It was a haven, a neighborhood touchstone, a place that had seen countless laughs, tears, and clinks of wine glasses over plates of pasta.

It was home.

I took a steadying breath, running a hand through my hair and straightening my shoulders. This was it. Every step I'd taken, every compromise, every late night at Vitello's—all of it had led to this moment. I wasn't just fighting to keep a building intact or an employer afloat. I was fighting for the life Louie and I had built within these walls, for the people who saw Vitello's as part of their own story.

The thought grounded me, and as I gripped the door handle, my fingers tightened with determination. I could do this. I would do this. The envelope in my hand held the funds that could buy us precious time. I knew it wasn't enough to cover everything, but it was a step, a lifeline, and sometimes that was all you needed to pull yourself out of the deep end. Louie would understand that, and together we'd make it work.

Pushing the door open, I walked inside, the familiar smells of garlic and basil wrapping around me like a comforting embrace. The restaurant was quiet, the afternoon lull casting shadows across the empty tables. I scanned the room, half expecting Louie to appear with his usual warm greeting. Today, though, I was the one bringing hope to Vitello's, and I wasn't about to let it slip through my fingers.

Louie sat alone at one of the corner tables, his gaze distant, hands folded in front of him on the table. The soft light streaming in through the windows cast shadows across his face, making the fine lines on his brow seem deeper, his usually bright eyes a little dimmer. He looked like he'd aged overnight, weighed down by the burden of Vitello's future. The sight tugged at something deep in my chest, and I felt a fresh surge of determination.

I took a breath and stepped forward, each footfall filled with purpose as I closed the distance between us. I couldn't wait to share the news — to let him know that, despite everything, there was still hope.

Clutching the envelope tighter, I pictured the relief in his face when he saw the cash, the spark of optimism that would return when he realized he didn't have to face this alone.

"Louie," I breathed, and his gaze shifted to me, the ghost of a smile lifting one corner of his mouth.

"Annie." His voice was as warm as always, but there was a sadness there that hadn't been before. "Didn't expect to see you so soon."

I smiled, unable to hold back the excitement bubbling up inside. "I — I have something for you. Something that might help." I practically skipped the last few steps, my fingers shaking as I extended the envelope to him. "It's not everything, but it's enough to keep Vitello's going a little while longer."

Louie's eyes widened as he looked at the envelope, his hand reaching out but pausing just before it touched the cash. He looked back up at me, surprise etched across his face, and for a second, a glimmer of hope danced in his gaze. The anticipation in my chest was electric.

This was it — this was the beginning of Vitello's next chapter.

With a shaky but determined breath, I placed the envelope of cash on the table in front of Louie. My hand trembled as I set it down, feeling the weight of this moment as he looked up at me, surprised.

"Louie," I started, my voice thick with emotion. "I sold my engagement ring. For Vitello's."

Louie's eyes widened, his mouth opening slightly, but no words came out. I took a breath and continued, the pounding in my chest urging me on.

"I know it doesn't cover everything," I said, my voice soft but steady, "but it's something. I couldn't just stand by and watch this place — your dream — go down without a fight. Vitello's is more than just a restaurant. It's community, it's… it's family." My voice wavered as I added, "I'm here to help, Louie. To do whatever it takes to keep this place open. We can find more ways. Together."

Louie stared at the envelope, his weathered hands hovering over it like he was afraid it might disappear. Then he looked back at me, gratitude and disbelief mingling on his face. "Annie," he murmured, his faint Italian accent thickening his voice. "You sold your engagement ring... for *this*?"

I nodded, swallowing the lump in my throat. "It didn't mean what I thought it did. But this place does."

He blinked, his eyes glistening, and for a moment, I thought I saw a tear shimmer in the corner of his eye. "You... you didn't have to do this, *cara mia*."

"But I wanted to," I replied, a fierce resolve building in me. "Vitello's gave me a place when I had nowhere else to go. It's my home as much as it's yours, Louie. And I want to help keep it alive."

Louie reached across the table, taking my hand in his, squeezing it tightly. "Thank you, Annie," he whispered, his voice thick with emotion. "I... don't know what to say."

Louie's eyes widened, and his mouth opened slightly as he looked down at the cash spread on the table, then back up at me. I'd never seen him at a loss for words, and it made my heart pound with anticipation.

His hands rested on the envelope as if grounding himself, his expression a mix of disbelief and awe. "Annie," he finally murmured, his voice soft, touched, almost like he didn't believe it. "You... you really did this?"

I nodded, feeling the last sliver of worry

slide away, replaced by a fierce hope. "Yes, Louie. I meant it when I said I'd do whatever it took. This place—it's everything. It deserves a fighting chance."

Louie's gaze softened, and I felt his pride and gratitude radiating from him. I'd gone all-in for Vitello's, and the relief on his face made it feel worth every bit. But he still hadn't said if it was enough, and I held my breath, waiting, silently praying that this would be enough to save us both.

Louie's sigh weighed heavily between us, filling the small gap of silence I hadn't known could hurt this much. He reached across the table, his hand trembling slightly as he took mine. "Annie," he murmured, his voice softer than I'd ever heard it. "I wish I could accept this, *tesoro*. I really do. But… it's too late."

The words took a moment to register, like a foreign language I'd have to translate to understand.

"Too late?" I repeated, almost disbelieving. I glanced down at the cash I'd placed on the table, still believing it could somehow be the miracle Vitello's needed. But Louie's somber gaze told me the truth I didn't want to hear.

He squeezed my hand gently. "I didn't want to tell you like this. I decided just this morning," he said, his face creased with a mix of sadness and resolution. "I signed the papers.

Vitello's... it's already sold."

My heart dropped, my thoughts scattering like dry leaves in a storm. "But Louie," I stammered, my voice barely above a whisper, "I sold my ring — Trent's ring. I was going to help... we were going to save Vitello's together."

A sad smile touched his lips. "Oh, Annie, I know how much this place means to you, and it means the world to me, too. But it was just... there was no other way. The bank, the debts... they don't wait."

I struggled to hold on to my composure as the weight of his words sunk in. All my plans, the dreams I'd had of running Vitello's side by side with him — it felt like sand slipping through my fingers. I'd come here ready to change everything, but reality had already changed the script. Louie's face softened as he released my hand, his own eyes glistening. "I'm sorry, *ragazza mia*. I never wanted it to end like this."

I stared at Louie, barely able to process his words. It felt as if I were trying to make sense of a bad dream, one that should have dissolved the moment I opened my eyes. But this wasn't a dream.

This was final.

My mind replayed every sleepless night, every frantic effort, every fleeting glimmer of hope I'd held onto to save Vitello's — and now, in one quiet moment, it was all gone.

The cash sat on the table between us, almost mocking in its weight. All the sacrifices, every painful step it had taken to bring that money here, felt utterly meaningless.

I'd given up so much — my engagement, my pride, even the last little piece of a life I'd once thought I wanted — all to save this place. To save Louie's place.

Our place.

And yet, it had slipped through my fingers before I even had a chance to hold it steady.

"Louie, why didn't you tell me?" I whispered, my voice laced with betrayal and heartbreak. I didn't mean to let it slip through like that, but it felt like every nerve inside me was fraying. "I would have done anything — anything to help you."

Louie's face crumpled, his own sadness apparent.

Curtis appeared from the kitchen, his dark face placid. He placed a big hand on my shoulder, but I shrugged it away.

"Now, come on, Annie. You know, sometimes in life, you got to pick your battles. And…well, some battles can't be won, no matter how much we love 'em." His words stung because they held a truth I hadn't wanted to face.

I forced myself to breathe, to steady my

shaking hands. This wasn't just losing a restaurant—it was losing a dream, a piece of myself. Everything I had fought for was wrapped up in those walls. And now, all I could do was watch it slip away, knowing my best wasn't enough.

Louie's voice softened, like he was sharing a secret he'd kept buried. "I know this is hard to understand, Annie, but I think… maybe it's time." He looked down, fingers tracing the worn wood of the table. "Eva and I… we've talked a lot about what comes next. She's been after me to travel with her, to see the world—Italy, especially. She says her hometown is like a dream." His eyes brightened with a hope that tugged at my heart.

I forced myself to listen, even as my heart twisted. Vitello's wasn't just his; it had become my dream, too. But here was Louie, looking like he'd finally found a way to let go, as if he was ready to close the book on the chapters I'd just started writing.

"I've been tied to this place for years, *più della metà della mia vita*—more than half my life." He smiled wistfully. "Maybe I've held on out of habit. But Annie, there's a whole world out there." He chuckled, soft and warm. "Eva, she says I'll love Florence, that I'll spend my days sipping espresso and eating *dolci*. Who am I to argue with that?"

His words, as sincere as they were, stung more than I could put into words. There was so much I wanted to say, to make him see how much this place meant to me, too. But I could see it in his eyes — the relief of a man who had finally let go of a weight that had bound him.

While I wanted to be happy for him, a hollow ache filled my chest, reminding me that his dream left little room for mine.

Louie kept talking, his words painting a picture of sunlit piazzas, winding Italian streets, and endless glasses of Chianti shared under the Tuscan sky. His voice held a rare lightness, as if some heavy, invisible weight had finally lifted. I felt the ache in my chest deepen, but now it was wrapped in something almost sweet — a strange mix of sadness and acceptance I hadn't expected.

"I know, *cara*, it seems sudden," he said, looking at me with a softness I rarely saw. "But there comes a point when you realize… holding on too tight can keep you from where you're supposed to be. Vitello's, she's been my life. But maybe it's time I start living for myself, *sì*?"

I managed a small nod, though my throat felt tight. This place had been my anchor, my dream, my everything — but it had been that for Louie, too. Only he'd given so much more. Maybe he deserved this next chapter, even if it left me behind. My fingers ran over the cash I'd laid on the table, feeling the hard-earned money now like a quiet, almost silly gesture. It was too late, too small in the face of a decision that felt like fate.

The weight of loss pressed into me, a hollowing realization that the Vitello's I'd loved was already gone, already drifting into memory. But there was something unexpectedly freeing in the acceptance, too. Maybe Louie was right. Maybe the world was bigger than this restaurant, this corner of town. For him, that world was in Italy, with Eva and a future he could build from scratch. For me...

Maybe my world was still waiting.

I took a breath, letting it settle into resolve, even as the ache lingered. Sometimes, letting go wasn't just an end — it was a start.

Louie nodded gently toward the dining room, his hand resting briefly on my shoulder. "Go on, *cara*. Take a last look around... say your goodbye." He gave me a wistful smile, then turned to the kitchen, disappearing into the shadows.

I stood alone, the quiet hum of the restaurant filling the space between my breaths. Vitello's was empty now, tables bare, chairs turned neatly, almost as if it were asleep. I took a slow walk around, tracing my fingers along the woodwork of each table, remembering the laughter, the clinking glasses, and the scent of freshly cooked pasta that had once filled this room.

Each step felt heavy, my mind flickering through scenes of shared meals and crowded dinner services. I could almost hear Louie calling out orders, the sound of pans clattering in the kitchen, the energy of a Saturday night rush. I lingered at one of the corner tables by the window where I'd spent hours jotting down recipe ideas, dreaming up dishes, imagining what I'd someday bring to this place. It was here that I'd first found myself as a chef, surrounded by people who believed in my love for food as much as I did.

When I reached the kitchen doorway, I paused, letting the memories settle. This was where I'd learned that cooking was more than just a job—it was a passion. Something that could make a person feel seen, understood, loved. Standing here, I felt a bittersweet pride—the kind that came from knowing this chapter had been beautiful, even if it was ending sooner than I'd hoped.

I turned back to the dining room, feeling a last wave of gratitude wash over me. Louie stood by the bar, his arms crossed, as he watched me with a soft smile. His eyes held the glimmer of a proud father, and for a moment, I struggled to find the right words.

How could I possibly sum up everything he'd

given me?

"Louie," I began, my voice catching. I took a breath and started again, "I just… I want you to know how grateful I am. You believed in me from the very beginning, when I hadn't even gone to culinary school and barely knew my way around a kitchen." I smiled, thinking back to all those early nerve-wracking shifts. "You taught me everything, from handling a dinner rush to making the perfect marinara. You've been more than a boss—you've been family."

Louie's face softened as he reached out and clasped my hand. "Annie, *cara mia*, don't make me tear up now," he said, his voice wavering just enough to make me smile. "You've always been part of this family. From the moment you walked in here, I knew you were special. This place… it was better because of you." He squeezed my hand. "And whatever you do next, it'll be better because of you, too."

His words sank in, bringing warmth to the ache in my chest. I felt a little steadier, a little braver. Knowing that Louie saw something in me, that he believed in my future, made saying goodbye just a bit easier.

"I'll never forget everything you taught me, Louie. *Grazie, davvero*," I said, my voice thick with emotion.

He pulled me into a hug, his embrace warm

and reassuring. "*Vai avanti,*" he murmured, his voice gentle. "Go forward. You've got a big future ahead of you, Annie."

I pulled back, giving him one last smile before stepping toward the door, ready to see where that future would take me.

I took a few steps, clutching my bag, and stopped, my emotions a tangled mess of grief and freedom and a heavy sense of loss. This was it — my connection to Vitello's was over. I'd poured so much of myself into this place, only to watch it slip away. The longer I stood there, the more the reality settled, replaced by something sharper, hotter.

Frustration.

A little spark lit in my chest, growing with each heartbeat. I'd sacrificed so much to save Vitello's, bending over backward and jumping through hoops, all while trying to balance Trent's expectations, the cooking competition, and my own dreams. I'd followed every rule, every unwritten social norm, hoping it would all magically work out if I just held on tightly enough. And here I was, empty-handed.

The feeling built, coursing through me with an energy I hadn't expected. For once, I was tired of playing it safe, tired of waiting for things to fall into place. I wanted to act — to do something bold, something that was just mine.

"Enough," I muttered under my breath, squaring my shoulders.

I spun back around, catching Louie just before he headed through the kitchen doors. My voice was louder than intended, a mixture of frustration and determination, startling him as he stopped in his tracks.

"Listen, Louie, I just… I need to know something," I said, crossing my arms tightly. "Whoever you sold Vitello's to—they need to understand what they're getting. They can't just come in and turn it into some trendy pop-up or knock it down for condos. This place has… it has a soul."

Louie raised his brows, a little bemused but listening patiently. "I did my best to make sure it's in good hands, *cara mia*," he said, a softness in his eyes.

"Good," I continued, feeling a surge of resolution. "Because I put my whole heart into this place, Louie. My heart and soul."

Louie started to respond, his eyes warm with understanding, but a voice interrupted from just behind me, low and familiar, with a touch of amusement.

"Well, hopefully not your *whole* heart."

Chapter Thirty-Three

Jordan

As Annie turned, her eyes locked on me, and for a brief moment, I saw her drop her guard, just the faintest hint of surprise softening her features. She blinked, her gaze shifting down to my hand—the old, worn key I held out for her.

"Jordan," she murmured, her voice a mix of shock and something else, maybe curiosity, maybe hope. For the first time since I'd stepped back into her life, she looked at me like she wasn't sure what to make of me.

Louie, who'd been watching our little exchange, stepped back, hands in his pockets, a slow, satisfied smile spreading across his face.

The old guy knew a thing or two about timing.

"I think," I said, keeping my tone steady even as my heart pounded harder than I'd like to admit, "this might belong to you."

Her eyes darted between me and the key, her usual confidence giving way to something else entirely. "What… what are you doing here,

Jordan?"

I shrugged, trying to play it casual. "I heard this place was going up for sale and thought, maybe, it was time to put down some roots."

The words came out softer than I'd intended, but I kept my gaze steady, watching the realization dawn in her eyes.

"You…" she whispered, clearly piecing it together.

I closed the space between us, and without another word, gently placed the key in her hand. She looked down at it, then back up at me, eyebrows furrowing as confusion washed over her face.

"Jordan… what is this?" she asked, her voice barely more than a whisper.

I bit back a grin, enjoying the moment more than I probably should have. The thrill of seeing her put the pieces together, knowing she hadn't yet realized what was happening—it was a satisfaction I hadn't felt in a long time. I gave a small nod toward the restaurant, holding my breath as I watched her.

"Why don't you tell me?" I prompted, unable to keep the excitement from my voice.

She shook her head, glancing between the key in her hand and Vitello's behind her, processing the possibilities. A flicker of something brightened in her eyes, but she forced it down, as if not daring to believe.

"This… no, that's impossible," she said, gripping the key more tightly. "Jordan, what did you do?"

"Oh, nothing much," I said, shrugging. "Just thought that some things… deserved another chance, that's all."

Her mouth fell open as the realization took full hold. "You *bought* Vitello's?" Her words were barely a whisper, her gaze piercing, as if she needed absolute confirmation.

I nodded, fighting to keep my tone light despite the intensity of the moment. "Thought maybe the place could use someone who really gets it, you know?" I let my smile soften as I added, "And someone who'll let you make all the Chicken Acapulco you want."

Annie looked down at the key again, her hand trembling slightly, and I could see a hundred emotions flickering across her face—surprise, gratitude, and something that looked an awful lot like joy.

I watched Annie, waiting for her to process what I'd just done. Her eyes widened as she looked down at the key in her hand, then back up at me, clearly stunned.

"I couldn't stand by and watch you lose this place, Annie," I said, keeping my voice steady, though my heart raced. "Vitello's… it's part of you, part of what you've built and dreamed about."

She blinked, as if still piecing everything together. Her fingers traced over the key, and I felt a rush of excitement. I'd wanted this moment for so long.

"I know I've been out of the loop," I admitted. "But Granny McGowan mentioned you might be facing a tough time with the restaurant." I paused, watching her expression soften. "And I thought, 'This is it. This is my chance to be there for her in a way that matters.' I just couldn't let this place disappear. Not if I could do something about it."

Her gaze lifted, her eyes searching mine, and I thought back to something Granny had told me once. I managed a small smile. "She reminded me that love sometimes means making room— giving someone the space to build something real. And that's what I want for you, Annie. To build this place into whatever you want it to be."

Annie's face softened as she looked at me, and in that quiet moment, I could feel the walls between us melt away.

Annie's eyes shimmered, her gaze fixed on the key in her hand as if it held the entire world. She opened her mouth to speak but stopped, pressing her lips together, holding back whatever wave of emotion had hit her. Her fingers tightened around the key, and I could see her shoulders tremble, just barely, as she looked up at me, eyes brimming.

"Jordan," she finally managed, her voice breaking a little with my name. She shook her head in disbelief, looking down at the key again and then back at me, as though trying to process that this wasn't some elaborate dream. "I… I don't even know what to say."

"You don't have to say anything," I whispered, taking a step closer. I could feel the intensity of the moment settle between us, that unspoken connection sparking to life. "I just wanted you to have this chance, Annie. To keep what matters most."

She let out a shaky breath, clutching the key so tightly her knuckles turned white. "This is… more than I could ever ask for," she whispered. "You didn't have to do this. But you did. And I—" She stopped, pressing her hand to her mouth as if trying to hold back a surge of emotion. "Thank you. Truly."

I felt my throat tighten, watching her stand there with her heart in her eyes. This wasn't just about Vitello's—it was about giving her a chance to reclaim everything she'd worked so hard to build. And seeing her, here and now, finally getting that chance…

It was better than any prize or title I'd ever

won.

"Annie," I said, my voice barely a whisper, "you don't have to thank me. I just wanted you to know I'm here. For whatever you need."

She met my gaze, her eyes shining with gratitude and something else—something that felt more real than anything between us ever had. At that moment, I knew.

This was where I was supposed to be.

I took a deep breath, mustering every ounce of courage I had. "And, well… since I sort of overheard you're single again…"

Annie's eyes widened, and her mouth opened slightly as if to say something, but she didn't. I was already in motion, lowering myself down on one knee, feeling the tile beneath me and the weight of the moment pressing in. Her gaze stayed locked on me, equal parts surprise and disbelief.

I gestured to the key in her hand. "I know it's not a ring," I said, my voice steady, though my heart felt like it was racing in place. "But it's definitely you. It's the place you've poured your heart and soul into. And it's the kind of place I've always seen you belong."

Annie's lips curved into the faintest smile, her eyes never leaving mine.

"So, I'm just kind of hoping," I continued, my words soft but sure, "that it can be an 'us.'"

For a moment, the world blurred away. The noise of the city outside, the clank of pots, even the creak of the door as Louie discreetly slipped into the kitchen — all of it faded. There was only her, looking down at me with the key in her hand, that beautiful hint of disbelief in her expression.

She swallowed, her voice barely a whisper. "Jordan, you're... serious?"

I nodded. "More serious than I've ever been."

A pause filled the space between us as she took a breath, her hand still clutching that key like it was a lifeline. She looked down at it, running her fingers along the worn metal, and then back up at me, her expression softening, a mix of wonder and warmth that told me everything I needed to know.

"So," I said, daring a smile, "what do you say? You up for cooking up some trouble? Together?"

"Mmmm, okay. But just so you know... I like it spicy." Annie's face broke into a grin so wide I thought my heart might burst. And before I could even brace myself, she flung herself at me, wrapping her arms around my neck and tackling me to the ground. We landed on the tile with a jolt, her laughter ringing out as she pressed her lips to mine in a kiss that felt like years of waiting and wondering were finally answered.

She kissed me fiercely, her hands in my hair, and I felt the world tilt as I wrapped my arms around her, pulling her closer. There was laughter and clapping nearby, and when we finally broke apart, breathless, I saw Louie peeking over the kitchen partition, a wide grin on his face. He clapped his hands and laughed, his deep, knowing chuckles filling the air.

"Ah, now that's *amore*!" he shouted, throwing his hands up. "I knew you two were somethin' special."

Curtis was standing just behind him, and to my surprise, he swiped at his cheek, brushing away a tear he didn't even try to hide. He just nodded at me, a silent, happy acknowledgment that made my throat tighten.

Annie looked down at me, her face alight with joy, her hair tumbling over her shoulder and brushing my cheek. "You have no idea how long I've been waiting to do that," she whispered, her eyes sparkling.

"Actually, I think I do," I replied, grinning up at her. "But if this is what happens, I'd wait all over again."

She laughed, resting her forehead against mine for a moment, both of us catching our breath.

Louie cleared his throat, gesturing grandly at the people gathering outside. "You two gonna keep puttin' on a show, or are you ready to open the doors and celebrate properly?"

Annie climbed off me, pulling me to my feet. She grasped my hand, a smile still tugging at her lips, and glanced over at Louie. "Only if you're buying the wine."

Louie laughed again, holding the door open with a flourish. "Anything for you, *bella ragazza*."

And with that, hand in hand, Vitello's was open for business, ready to start a new chapter.

One where love was always on the menu.

What's Next? A Sneak Peek at Marley's Next Rom-Com!

Loved Annie & Jordan? You're going to ADORE what's coming next! Keep reading for an exclusive first chapter from Marley's next book!

The Kat's Meow
Release Date:
May 1, 2025

Preorders Open April 2nd!

Get a reminder when it's available—Join the Foxes & Flirts newsletter. Scan the QR to join now!

Or sign-up at
https://bit.ly/marleyfoxauthor

👉 Turn the page to start reading Chapter One now!

The Kat's Meow

MARLEY FOX

"Lusty loins?" Gimme a break, Kat! Why do you read this garbage?" Gina popped her nuclear green gum for the thousandth time as she plopped the offending romance back in the newsstand display.

I snatched the book back, trying to ignore my best friend, which I almost accomplished once I got past the five-inch stilettos, snakeskin skirt, and hair color of the week. Today's shade was a startling hue of yellow. Not blonde. Yellow. As a canary's...

I shook my head. Apparently, Madame Maxine's House of Beauty didn't have a strict employee dress code. My therapy clients, however — or their owners, at least — expected a little more... discretion in apparel.

I shifted my Prada bag as my tall, skinny, no-foam latte threatened to deluge the stack of periodicals below me. I didn't miss the scowl of the newsstand proprietor.

"Because. In the end, you always know the girl and the guy wind up together," I stated matter-of-factly. A sour memory wrinkled my brow. "Not like real life."

Real life was messy. Romance novels had guaranteed happy endings. But as long as my nose was buried in a Lily LaFleur book, I could believe — if only for a few hundred pages — that the right guy existed.

Gina threw her hands up in the air. "Oh, come on! You're not still on over that idiot again, are you?"

I shot her a pout. "You try being dumped by your fiancé and then tell me how you feel."

"The man was as exciting as a wet dish rag, Kat. Good riddance, if you ask me."

"Well, I'm not."

The tough expression on Gina's face softened — or maybe the Manhattan summer was just melting her concealer. Either way, she placed a gentle hand on my shoulder. "You deserve so much better."

I managed a small grin. She was right. I did deserve better. And I knew exactly where to find the perfect guy. "Excuse me, do you have the new Lily LaFleur romance?"

The proprietor sneered. "Lady, this ain't no Barnes and Noble."

I smiled sweetly. "Could you just check for

me, please?"

The man grumbled something about "dames" and started digging through his inventory.

Gina rolled her eyes at me. I stuck out my tongue and gave her a hearty Bronx cheer which she returned in kind.

"What the hell is a loin, anyways?" Gina's face puckered. "I mean, is it like them chops you get at Gennaro's Market? 'Cause, I gotta be honest with you — cold, dead meat don't exactly carbonate my hormones, if you know what I'm sayin'."

"Here you go, lady. That'll be ten fifty." The newsstand guy shoved the book toward me, eyes darting nervously in both directions.

Guess he didn't want to be seen with his hands on the tanned, well-muscled chest of the book's hero on the cover.

Me, on the other hand…

Money and book exchanged hands eagerly. Gina and I started walking toward the train.

I immediately buried my nose in chapter one.

"Dark and mysterious, the night promised passion." I sighed and clutched the book to my chest.

Gina groaned. She grabbed my arm, pulling me to a halt. "Okay, look. I'm going to offer my professional opinion here."

I tilted my head. "Professional opinion? You're a hairdresser."

"In the boroughs, that makes me Sigmund friggin' Freud. You keep waiting for some impossibly incredible guy to sweep you off your feet, you'll wind up like one of them dotty old blue-haired broads that always smells like baby powder and tuna and has, like, a bazillion cats." Gina cocked her head. "You could pull off the blue-haired thing, though."

I pouted. "My hair is brown. I only have one cat. And I'm not waiting for *some* guy. I'm just waiting for, well, the *right* guy."

"This is us," Gina stopped at the subway entrance. "You coming?"

"I think I'm gonna walk. Maybe stop in the park and do a little reading." I glanced at the bag in my hand.

Gina patted my face with five candy-apple red talons. "Life ain't a romance novel, Kat. The happy-ever-after isn't always on page 325. It's out there." She gestured and looked intently into my eyes. "Promise me you're going to look for it."

I shrugged.

She grabbed me by both shoulders. "Promise!"

I chuckled. "Okay, okay. I'll keep my eyes open."

Gina grinned. "Alright! That's what I'm talkin' about!" She stole a glance at her watch. "Oh, crap. I'm gonna miss the train!" She planted a quick kiss on my cheek, her heels clicking on the pavement as her mincing steps took her toward the steps. "Go knock 'em dead."

Loved what you read? There's more where that came from! Be the first to know when *The Kat's Meow* is up for pre-order (plus get VIP extras!) — join my Foxes & Flirts list at **www.marleyfox.com**.

Stay Foxy & Never Miss a Flirty Read

💙 Love swoon-worthy romance, laugh-out-loud banter, and flirty, feel-good reads?
💙 Join the *Foxes & Flirts* newsletter for exclusive perks!

What's in it for you?

💙 A special bonus scene from *Cooking Up Trouble!*
💙 Early sneak peeks of my next book (before anyone else!)
💙 Exclusive giveaways, rom-com fun, and insider bookish gossip!

Scan the QR to join now and grab your freebie!

Or sign-up at
https://bit.ly/marleyfoxauthor

Who's Behind the Flirt?

Marley Fox is an award-winning writer with a passion for mixing sharp wit, swoon-worthy romance, and high-stakes drama. With an award-winning background in storytelling, she brings heart and humor to every page. When she's not writing, she's indulging in her love of Italian food, competitive baking shows, and café-hopping for research (or so she claims).

Let's keep the flirt going! Follow Marley online:

Website: www.marleyfoxauthor.com
Instagram: @marleyfoxauthor
Facebook: @marleyfoxauthor

Be a Fox, Leave a Review!

Huge thanks to my incredible Foxes & Flirts for taking this journey with Annie & Jordan! Your support means the world.

Reviews mean everything to authors like me! If Annie and Jordan's story made you laugh, swoon, or crave a plate of Chicken Acapulco, I'd be beyond grateful if you shared your thoughts.

Your review doesn't have to be long—just a few words about what you loved (or which scene made you snort-laugh in public) can help more readers find this book!

Leave a little love on Amazon, Goodreads, or BookBub—it's like a virtual hug for an author.

Thank you for being part of Marley Fox's Foxes & Flirts! Your support keeps the rom-com magic alive. 🖤